THE CIRCLET TREASURY OF EROTIC WONDERLAND:

EROTIC TALES OF ALICE AND BEYOND

EDITED BY J. BLACKMORE

For more information contact:
Riverdale Avenue Books
5676 Riverdale Avenue
Riverdale, NY 10471
www.riverdaleavebooks.com

Design by www.formatting4U.com
Cover by Scott Carpenter
Digital ISBN: 978-1-62601-282-0
Print: 978-1-62601-283-7
Originally published as *Like the Knave of Hearts*, edited by J. Blackmore, Circlet Press, 2010, and *Like a Vorpal Blade*, edited by J. Blackmore, Circlet Press, 2011.
First edition June 2016

Table of Contents

Introduction

We're all mad here. We were drawn to Alice as children. We agreed that a book without pictures or conversations is seriously lacking, and that even insanity has a certain logic to it. We grew up with Alice, and she has grown up too. These are stories of a Wonderland that has become darker, sexier, more complicated and infinitely more wonderful in the telling. In the first half of the book, five authors tell tales of a world where dreams are real and always have happy endings. They believe that the journey through this place leaves the wanderer richer, wiser and satisfied.

Morwenna Drake imagines what life may be like for the royal court of the White King and Queen. The world through the looking glass is likened to a giant chessboard, and those who dare it must keep their wits about them. "Lily White" tells the story of a young princess whose aimless life is transformed by a walk through the squares. As we journey with Lily, we too learn the six valuable rules one must follow to balance fantasy and pleasure with everyday life.

But we must return to Alice. How could she possibly have coped with growing up and away from Wonderland? Alex Picchetti thinks that she could have left a bit of herself behind there, a mirror image of her more mature thoughts and wishes. "A World of Her Own" is about Alice's very grown-up adventures. Married now, she occasionally slips back through the glass to lose herself in exotic pleasures. Refreshed by these experiences, she can go on with her sedate Victorian life.

However, Alice could also have forced herself to forget Wonderland, out of fear or a need to fit in. Holly Abair thinks that Alice may have learned to hide her longing. In "Tarts and Tea," Alice has fled from her dreams for years, but is given the chance to return to them on the eve of her wedding. The world she finds has been transformed by her neglect into a land of misery and nightmares, but there is still hope, because that is one thing that Alice has never given up.

Gary Westfahl reminds us that Alice was a logical, pragmatic child; selfish and wise, generous and mocking. He can't imagine she would be so very different as a woman and, maybe as a prank, sets her down willy-nilly in a lost chapter of her past. "A Wasp, a Wig and a Wanton Woman" is a ridiculous, poignant and whimsical story that, for all of its unrepentant debauchery, strongly harkens back to Carroll's precise silliness.

Verity Penvenen suggests that Alice has already had her adventures, and instead takes one of us on a whirlwind tour of Wonderland. Natasha, in "Wonders Wild and New," thinks she has simply bought a bit of nostalgic comfort from a mysterious bookseller on a horrible day. But falling asleep while reading *Alice* sends her on an adventure far beyond her comfort zone and miles away from the destination she thought she was seeking.

But, *beware the Jabberwock, my son...*

So says Lewis Carroll in his lyrical poem. Here he hints that he has not been telling us the whole story of Wonderland; that dangerous beasties are hiding just out of sight in every scene of Alice's adventures. This poem begins with a chant of precise nonsense and takes the reader through fear and murder, and back to nonsense again. For the authors in the second half of the book, this is the true face of Wonderland, and the nightmares it produces are the stories that they must tell.

The Queen of Hearts is the apparent ruler of Alice's dreams. She is hot-tempered, bloodthirsty and ultimately balanced by the persistent shadow of the King. But a Wonderland without Alice is a Wonderland cut loose from its center, and the Queen without her King is rage cut away from mercy. Theresa Sand takes us into the political world of the Court of Hearts, seen through the eyes of Alice's doppelganger, Mary Anne. "If This Be Not Love, It Is Madness" examines forbidden desire, and the dangers of love, stood starkly against the background of death.

The power of obsession is how it lives under the skin, crawling, writhing, driving to seek its object. Having fucked her way through Wonderland, Alice finds herself on the wrong side of the rabbit hole in Bernie Mojzes's "A Perfect Creature." Shunned by a lover who seemed made for her, Alice tries to ease her longing the only way she knows how. Her attempts fall somewhere between desperation and madness.

Madness is not funny. The whimsy of Wonderland sometimes makes us forget the terror of insanity. Alice knows what it means to lose herself, and building up a barrier of sanity is only one way to deal with it. In "Waking," ADR Forte tells us the story of a modern Alice leading a double life. She is content to wear a mask, sleepwalking through her days, until a man from her past meets her through the mirror and forces her to face who and what she truly is.

Wonderland doesn't always wait for us to visit. In moments of despair, the shadows may move, and we may be met in the darkness by everything we try to deny. Alex Picchetti drags us deep underground to a decadent, macabre carnival in "Midway Rides." There, all the most disturbing of Carroll's characters run a series of attractions that lay open the soul and cost nothing less than your life as you know it.

The Jabberwock is never fully described. The Jabberwock is indescribable. The Jabberwock only has power when you think of him, face him, become him. It's the Summer of Love, and a Vietnam vet lands in a little resort town, looking for answers to questions he hasn't asked. "The Boiling Sea" by Angela Caperton is the story of his journey from war to the peace that can only come when one has passed all one's tests. On the way, he will come under the power of a magician, face a monster and learn to wield his Vorpal blade.

In our first five stories we visited Wonderland as grown-ups, able at last to face imagination as our full sexual selves, and reveling in it. In these last five, we face madness, despair, destruction and death. But, always, always, wonder wins. After all, we are, ultimately, in control of our nightmares, and they have much to teach us. They are the darker half of our desires, and as utterly necessary as breathing. And as utterly inevitable as the cessation of breath.

J. Blackmore
August 2015

Lily White

Morwenna Drake

"You can't be a Queen, you know, till you've passed the proper examination. And the sooner we begin it, the better. "
—Red Queen to Alice, *Through the Looking Glass*

Beginnings

Lily opened the storeroom door a crack and peeked out. The corridor was deserted. She paused to give a brief wink to the pageboy lying prostrate on a sack of corn, and his flushed face split into a huge grin as he winked back.

Stepping out into one of the minor corridors of the castle, Lily closed the door silently behind her. With one final glance in both directions, she began walking regally toward her drawing room in the east wing.

Just as she was reaching the door to the great hall, her foot snagged on something. Glancing down, Lily realized her stocking had fallen down around her slipper. Muttering, she bent down and pulled the stocking back up her leg. She took care this time in securing the ribbon round the top of her thigh before letting her gown fall back down. An impudent whistle made her turn sharply.

Leaning against one of the huge marble pillars of her father's castle was a man she knew well. The Royal Carpenter was a man who knew many secrets. His work took him all over the castle, as well as to every part of the land, and the things he heard could bring the country to ruin, or save it. No one was quite sure which. And now it appeared he knew one of Lily's secrets.

"Carpenter," Lily said imperiously. She tried not to let the guilt on her face show. If anything, he would be the criminal, for spying on a member of the royal family.

"Princess Lily," said the Carpenter. "I do believe I have just seen a part of you which no other commoner in the realm has done. Or, perhaps not..." He left the sentence hanging as he glanced back the way she had come. Lily followed his gaze and cursed silently when she saw the storeroom door open a crack.

The pageboy, taken on by the Royal Butler not more than a month ago, was as yet naïve in the ways of the court. He was lacking in the art of subterfuge, so when he saw Lily he waved impishly and hurried off.

"Not the most subtle," commented the Carpenter with a raised eyebrow. He had been hidden from the boy's line of sight by the pillar, but the Carpenter craned his neck to watch the young lad hurrying away, adjusting his breeches as he went. Lily rolled her eyes.

"I am sure I can trust you with such a secret, Carpenter," she said. She tried to adopt the authoritative tone her father, the White King, used when he was not to be disobeyed. The Carpenter merely chuckled lightheartedly.

"I do have a reputation for secrets," he said, his eyes twinkling with a dark light. He moved closer to her. "Perhaps I could share one with you. Would that prospect tempt you, Princess Lily?" He reached out, as if to stroke a stray wisp of hair from her face, but then hesitated at the last second and withdrew his hand. Lily could barely breathe with the anticipation that squeezed her heart.

"What would tempt me would be to find myself alone in a storeroom with you rather than a silly little pageboy," Lily said boldly. The corner of her lip curled up into the seductive smile she had been practicing in the bronze mirror that very morning.

"Your time would be better spent in the company of Sir Bruno," replied the Carpenter, his voice low. Lily snorted derisively.

"The White Rabbit? I think not."

"It is cruel to call people by such names, Princess," the Carpenter said reprovingly. Lily lifted her chin defiantly.

"It is merely how the rest of the court names him," she replied. "And, yes, I would see Sir Bruno, if his talents were to my liking. I find my tastes are more... refined."

It was the Carpenter's turn to be derisive. "I

would hardly call a pageboy with more in his trousers than in his head a 'refined' choice, Princess." The Carpenter shook his head sadly. "You will never reach the Sixth Square if you choose such companions."

The Carpenter began to turn away, but Lily's hand snapped out and caught his arm. She was momentarily taken aback by the hard muscles she felt beneath her fingertips.

"The Sixth Square—what is that?" she demanded. As he turned back, she saw the mischievous curl of his lip, the slightly raised eyebrow. She realized that he had baited a trap and she had fallen straight in.

"Why, Princess, if you do not know, I don't know if I should be the one to tell you," he replied innocently. "After all, the making of a queen is not a matter to be taken lightly."

"You can make me a queen?" Lily asked. As one of eight children, this boast appealed to her.

"I can show you the path, but you must follow it," said the Carpenter. "Would you like to see that much?" Lily answered with a vigorous nod. He grinned.

Lily followed the Carpenter out of the castle. As a child, she had thought she had played in all the corridors and alcoves, but the Carpenter took her through secret doors and down cobwebbed passages that she had never even guessed existed.

They finally emerged outside the castle walls with the dark forest stretching ahead of them for miles in all directions. Lily was tingling with the exhilaration of being somewhere she knew she should not be, with someone she probably should not be with. Probably.

As the Carpenter headed down the slope toward the tree line, Lily called out, "Wait! I really shouldn't go in there. Papa will murder me if he finds I've strayed into the forest."

The Carpenter turned round and stalked back, his eyes fixed on Lily. She quavered a little under his gaze, as a mouse might shiver when a cat stares into its nest.

"A queen in her own right would not be so fearful of her own kingdom," he said.

"I am not a queen."

"And you never will be if you don't come with me. What are you, Princess? Second youngest? Nowhere near a queen at all. If you want to stay here, you may do so, but I am going." With that, the Carpenter turned and headed back down the slope.

Lily hesitated, close to wringing her hands with indecision. She wanted so desperately to go with the Carpenter, to learn what he had to teach her, yet she feared the consequences. She shivered at the thought that he might try to accost her in the forest, force her up against a tree, and ravish her. Such delicious imaginings made her decision.

As he reached the shadow of the trees, the Carpenter turned and waited, his strong hands resting on his sturdy hips. As Lily approached him, she tried to mimic the stride her mother, the White Queen, used when she strode up the great hall. Yet her small teeth biting her pink lip gave away her nervousness.

The Carpenter nodded approvingly when she was beside him, triumph gleaming in his eyes. She had shown that she would follow him anywhere, and Lily felt a flutter of nervousness in her stomach at the power she was giving him.

"I am going into the forest with a man whose name I don't even know," Lily said. The Carpenter raised his eyebrow.

"Well," he mused, "I'm not just a Carpenter but a Jack of All Trades, so you can call me Jack."

"Lead on then, Jack," Lily said. Jack made a brief bow and then led her into the wood.

Rule One

The Carpenter led Lily some way into the forest before he stopped and turned. He wore a serious expression, so Lily assumed an attentive one.

"Now, Lily," he began in the manner of a stern teacher, "before you can become queen, there are certain rules to be learned. If you don't know and adhere to the six rules I am going to show you, then your rule will quickly falter."

"Does Mother adhere to them, then?" Lily asked with interest.

A smile flickered over Jack's face. "Why, of course," he said. "I showed her just the same as I am showing you now."

Lily gaped. It was on the tip of her tongue to ask in astonishment just how old he was, but then it occurred to her that this would appear rude, so she kept her peace.

Besides, she reasoned as she followed behind him, *his mind is still sharp and his body is still lithe and toned—oh, how toned—so what does it matter if he's as old as time?*

The Carpenter paused suddenly, and Lily nearly

ran into him. He turned to her and gestured that she go first. Lily moved forward cautiously. A row of trees stood before her, so covered in ivy and honeysuckle and other creepers that it seemed as if a curtain hung between the trunks.

Very carefully, Lily parted the living curtain before her and stepped through. She found herself in a clearing, the trees lining each side in four straight lines, effectively forming a square. Yet it was not this fact that made Lily's jaw drop.

The grass within the square was itself arranged into squares, sixty-four of them. There were people standing on some of the squares, dressed in a strange assortment of clothing. One woman wore a fabulous jeweled gown cut so low that her heavy breasts seemed poised on the verge of exposing themselves whenever she moved. A tiara glittered on her head, flashing as she wiggled her hips provocatively. Two squares in front of her and one to the right was a man wearing a knight's helmet and nothing else. He carried a shield on one arm and a lance in the other. His dark eyes were filled with lust as he watched the woman in the bejeweled gown. Lily heard the rustle of undergrowth as Jack stepped up behind her.

"It's a chessboard," she exclaimed with surprised delight. "Only, with real people rather than pieces. But I don't understand what those people are doing." Lily pointed to a dozen couples who were at the edge of the grass-board, coupling or rutting or just lying entwined.

"Those are the pieces that were lost during the game. See?" He gestured to one couple. "Bishop takes Rook." Lily stared at a woman with jet-black hair who was kneeling on all fours. She wriggled and moaned as a man in a miter thrust into her from behind.

"What kind of lesson is this?" Lily asked. A familiar heat was beginning to fill her as she watched the various acts of pleasuring taking place around the board. "Is it a lesson that I shouldn't play chess?"

"You can join in, if you want," called the woman in the luxurious gown. "We need another pawn." Lily shook her head shyly. The woman gave a disappointed sigh, which turned into a shriek of surprise as the knight closed the distance between them and leaped upon her. Lily gaped as he threw up her skirts and mounted her.

"Knight takes Queen," said the Carpenter over the woman's cries of delight.

"She's not a queen," said Lily scornfully, following Jack as he moved away. "I would have recognized her if she was."

"Well, you're not a queen either—yet," replied Jack. He stopped at the edge of the square. Lily obediently stopped too. "Rule One," announced Jack, raising a finger, "is that it's all a game. Anyone can—and will—play. You must always think three moves ahead if you don't wish to be soundly buggered."

Lily frowned. "That sounds more like three rules than one to me," she said. "Are they all going to be like this?"

Jack grinned. "Would you like to find out?" he asked.

Rule Two

The Carpenter gestured for Lily to go ahead once more.

"Can't I go that way?" asked Lily, pointing to the right.

"No, pawns can only go forward or diagonally," replied Jack.

"I'm not a pawn," replied Lily coldly, putting her hands on her hips and pouting. She made sure it was an alluring pout.

"You are a pawn," said Jack decisively. "You've five more rules and five more squares to go until you become queen. So, if you're ready..." He gestured again. Lily held her head in the air and marched forward into the second square. However, when she saw what it contained, she tried to back out again. As she took a step backward, she felt the solid bulk of Jack behind her. His chest was firm and muscled against her shoulders, and she was surprised to feel the hard length of his shaft pressing against her soft buttocks.

"What's the matter?" he asked her.

"It's the White King," whispered Lily, pointing to the man with the salt-and-pepper beard sitting in the center of the square. "It's my father."

"So?" replied Jack unconcernedly. "He's far too busy to notice you." Lily saw that he was right. The White King was sitting on a large wooden throne, much like the one he had in the castle. He was reading a lengthy scroll of parchment, his brow furrowed in concentration, completely oblivious to their presence.

"So I see," said Lily with mild amusement. "Only the King could find entertainment in paper and work when there's a whole wicked game of chess going on such a short way away."

"Oh, that is the price of kingship," said Jack. "Always business before pleasure. It could drive one mad if not for Rule Two."

"Which is?"

"Always find a way of turning your business into pleasure," Jack said with a knowing smirk. Lily was about to question him when the King held up his parchment. A servant scuttled out of nowhere to relieve him of it.

"Fetch me paper, ink, quill, and something to rest them on," the King demanded. The servant bowed and hurried away, returning immediately with the paper, ink, quill, and a young woman. Lily watched with astonishment as the woman knelt down on all fours in front of the White King. He placed the ink on her shoulders and the paper on her back.

With a look of concentration, the King dipped the quill into the ink and began to write. Lily stared up at Jack in astonishment.

"I swear he just uses tables at home," she said in a whisper.

"Undoubtedly," Jack said. "This forest isn't about

normality, Lily. It's where people come to find themselves and the pleasures they desire."

Lily turned back to see that the White King had paused in his writing. As he stared thoughtfully into space, she saw that one of his hands had drifted down to the woman's breast and he was idly stroking it, as if such motion was an aid to thought. The woman was biting her lip, trying not to giggle or sigh. Lily could see that there were ink stains around her nipple.

As the woman let out a short sigh, Lily felt her own nipples harden with desire, pressing against her dress. Behind her, Jack shifted his weight a little and his erection brushed against her again. It sent a delightful shiver down her spine.

The kneeling woman gave her own little shudder and upset the inkpot, which was resting on her back. The King looked down as it fell to the floor, splattering ink all over his paper.

"Damn woman—keep still!" he said as he gave her a short smack on her naked arse. The woman squeaked a mixture of pleasure and pain before trying to hold still. The King tutted as he rescued the ink-pot, then went back to writing.

"I think we should leave his majesty to it," whispered Jack in Lily's ear. "We still have four more lessons to go."

Rule Three

Lily led the Carpenter out of the second square and into the third. Even before the ivy had fallen back in place behind them, Lily was almost deafened by a deep, booming voice.

"Carpenter!"

"Gideon!" cried Jack in reply. He walked past Lily to embrace a very rotund man lying on a sedan chair. The man pushed off a nubile young woman who had been lying asleep on top of him, and she hit the ground, waking up with a disgruntled squeak. Jack turned and beckoned to Lily.

"Ah," said Gideon as Lily approached somewhat shyly, "you must be Lily. Do you know who I am?"

"Yes, you're the Walrus," replied Lily before she could stop herself. As she threw a hand over her mouth in horror, Gideon simply threw back his head and guffawed. His prominent jowls shook with the force of his mirth.

"I see that tact is not one of the lessons you're teaching her today, Carpenter," Gideon said, wiping tears of laughter from his eyes. Jack merely grinned in response. Gideon turned back to address Lily. "Yes, young lady. There are some who call me that—on account of my large whiskers, no doubt." He winked at her then, and Lily smiled politely, looking attentive.

"And are you my lesson, sir?" she asked.

Gideon beamed good-naturedly, his little eyes being momentarily obscured by fleshy wrinkles. "Indeed I am, young lady."

"And what lesson is that?" asked Lily patiently.

Gideon waved a hand in the air, imitating a regal pose. "Why, charm."

"Charm?" asked Lily, somewhat disbelieving.

"But of course," cut in Jack. "Do not let your eyes deceive you, Lily. This man could charm even the most stubborn lady out of her stockings."

"Really?" asked Lily. "He doesn't look like he could." Then she cursed aloud at the stupidity of being rude to him again yet again. Jack frowned at her, but Gideon merely chuckled heartily.

"Perhaps not, young lady, but appearances can be deceptive. After all, who would have realized that a proper and polite young girl like yourself knew such a word as the one you just uttered?" Lily blushed furiously at her indiscretion, but Gideon just waggled his finger. "Although, no doubt by the time our Carpenter has finished with you, there'll be a whole lot more that you will have learned."

Gideon nudged Jack in the ribs and winked. When Lily saw the glint in Jack's eyes at the jest, she gave a shiver of delicious anticipation. The small, intimate space between her legs was beginning to tingle, the flesh becoming slick.

"You mentioned charm?" Lily asked, suddenly

anxious to move the lesson along.

"Why indeed!" cried Jack, eager to sing his friend's praises. "There is no one so charming in the kingdom as Gideon here. He could charm the moon down from the skies if he needed it to penetrate a lady's skirts."

"Or a gentleman's pantaloons," added the Walrus.

"No one is immune to Gideon," Jack said, patting his friend affectionately on the shoulder. "Why, when we were visiting the harbor just the other day, Gideon got through a whole family of shell-seekers, didn't you? While I only managed two sisters who were cockle-picking."

"That was a day," replied Gideon with a wistful smile. "I remember it was the father who was the most surprised..." Lily placed her hands on her hips, feeling it was proper for her to be outraged at such lewdness.

"The Walrus and the Carpenter, what a pair you make," she said. "They should make a ballad out of the two of you."

"Only if it's very rude," replied Gideon.

Lily frowned. "I'm not seeing much evidence of charm," she said.

"Then watch and learn," replied Gideon, heaving his great bulk off the sedan. Jack came to stand next to Lily, just close enough that his arm brushed hers. The touch of his skin lit a fire in her belly, which she tried to ignore.

Gideon walked over to the young woman whom he had so unceremoniously pushed off him earlier. She sat in the corner, her knees drawn up to her chin, pouting. Lily saw Gideon draw her to her feet and wrap one of his arms around her waist. She tried to push him away, but not very hard. Gideon leaned to whisper something in her ear. Lily was too far away to hear his words, but she saw the woman's lips curl slowly from a downward sulk into a seductive smile.

After a few moments, the woman nodded and allowed Gideon to lead her back to the sedan. Ignoring Jack and Lily, Gideon laid the woman down on it before opening her legs and kneeling between them. He bent his head to kiss her knee, then traced a line with his lips up the inside of her thigh. The woman groaned with anticipation as Gideon kissed to the edge of her silken curls and then gasped with pleasure when he placed his mouth over her bud.

Lily watched as Gideon reached up to squeeze and tease the woman's breasts while his tongue continued to draw circles over her clitoris. Lily could feel the dampness between her own thighs as the woman writhed beneath Gideon's lips.

"Rule Three," said Jack in a low voice. "Know how to charm those around you, and you will encounter no resistance. Be a charming queen and everyone will love you and do as you say."

Gideon lifted his head, his chin slick with saliva and juices, to add, "Sometimes, your tongue can be your greatest ally, however you choose to use it." Then he gave her a truly lascivious wink before he turned and plunged his face back into the woman's soft center, sucking noisily. The woman's gasps and groans followed them as they made their way into the fourth square.

Rule Four

As Lily stepped into the fourth square clearing, her heart was beating fast. Arousal was slowly seeping through her body, coloring her skin and making her loins ache with need. Every time Jack put a hand at the base of her back to guide her way, his touch sent fire racing through her blood. But Lily was instantly distracted when she saw who inhabited the fourth square.

"It is the Red King," she said in surprise. She had seen him at banquets, speaking in serious tones to her father, but she had never been so close to him before.

He stood wearing nothing but his long cape of office, made of deep scarlet velvet and trimmed with ermine. His crown was set to one side, next to his scepter, and instead he held a small, thin square of wood. The Red King stood with his back to them, but when he moved Lily saw that a woman was tied to the tree in front of him. She was completely naked, and her long, red hair tumbled down to her waist. Her hands were stretched up, manacled to the branch above her.

"Who is that?" Lily whispered to Jack, pointing at

the woman. At that moment, the King brought the wooden paddle down in a stinging slap against the woman's buttocks. Her cry was one of pain, but it ended with a moan of intense pleasure. "Who is it?" asked Lily again, aghast.

"That is the Red Queen," Jack replied.

"No!" breathed Lily in shock. She remembered the Red Queen—a tall, strikingly beautiful woman who, it was well-known, was the real power behind the Red Throne. While the Red King's subjects may obey him, everyone knew it was the Red Queen they feared the most.

"Rule Four," said Jack as the Red King delivered another blow to his restrained wife's bare buttocks. "A queen may often have to rule contrary to her nature. A weak queen must appear strong to prevent rebellion, while a willful queen must allow herself to be ruled occasionally or risk disaffecting her subjects."

As Lily watched, the King continued to deliver his blows with cries such as "Is that what you want, Your Majesty?" and the Queen's arse began to redden. Lily felt sorry for the woman at first, until she realized the Red Queen arched her hips and eagerly raised her buttocks to meet each blow.

"What kind of pleasure does she get from that?" asked Lily in puzzlement. Without a word, Jack raised his hand and smacked it across Lily's own rear. She cried out in alarm as pain blossomed across her skin, but then something deeper began to burn.

"Oh, I see," she replied, somewhat sheepishly as the heat in her buttocks matched the fire that was beginning to blaze in her sex. Jack grinned, and out of the corner of her eye, Lily saw his cock twitch slightly as it strained against his breeches.

"Shall we move on to the fifth?" Jack asked lightly. Lily nodded and followed him across the square. They passed to the right of the Red King and Queen. Before she stepped through the hanging foliage, Lily glanced aside to see that the Red King had cast aside his paddle and had instead entered the Red Queen from behind.

The Red Queen was pressed against the tree trunk in what seemed to Lily a most uncomfortable manner as the Red King forged in and out of her, both of them wearing a look of ecstasy.

"I guess it takes all sorts to make a queen," Lily murmured to herself before stepping through into the next square.

Rule Five

"Here is someone you're sure to know," said Jack as Lily stepped into the fifth square behind him. Lily found it hard to see to whom Jack was referring since the square in front of her was filled with a writhing mass of limbs. Then a head poked out of the fray and grinned at them.

"Hello, Carpenter," said Sir Bruno. He disentangled himself from a blonde woman who was trying to fasten her lips around his erect cock. She muttered in frustration as he pushed her away, but turning round she found another willing member to feast upon.

Sir Bruno, the White Rabbit, came toward them with a winning smile. Lily had to shut her mouth as she stared at the length of him stretching toward her. She had seen many cocks in her time, but she had never witnessed one of such length or girth.

"So the stories are true," she whispered to Jack beside her, but not quietly enough to escape Bruno's ears.

"It depends on which stories you are referring to," he said. "If you mean my size, which would put the

King's finest stallion to shame, then you can see the truth for yourself." He leaned forward and fixed his sparkling, brown eyes on hers. "But if you mean," he said in a lower voice, "whether my promiscuities live up to my name of 'rabbit,' then I suggest you join me in a little demonstration."

Lily was speechless. Many dark and cold winter nights, she had lain in her bed and imagined the White Rabbit heating her chilled skin with kisses and riding her so hard that the sweat poured off her. Yet now that she was faced with him, suddenly the prospect looked less inviting. There was something about the way the man held himself that was distasteful to her. His brazen looks and the way he leaned toward her gave Lily the distinct impression that he thought only about what was between her legs.

"Lily is here to learn a lesson," said Jack. Lily noticed that he stepped toward her slightly, imperceptibly placing himself a little bit more between Lily and Bruno. She was glad of it. Bruno looked at Jack quizzically.

"Lesson?" he asked.

Jack turned to Lily. "Prince Bruno is an example of your fifth rule of the day," he said.

"Prince Bruno?" she asked, astonished. She turned to the White Rabbit. "You're a prince?"

"Certainly," Bruno replied with a deep bow. "The second eldest of five, but my parents sent me from their kingdom."

"Why?" Lily asked.

"Because my talents drew me in other directions," Bruno replied, looking down at himself meaningfully.

"A passion like mine should not be denied, yet my parents did not believe that skills such as those I possessed would make me a good king. So I was sent away. But such talk is dull, young Lily. Would you care to join us instead?" he asked, holding his hand out to her.

She shook her head, and Bruno gave her a regretful look, but turned away without another word. He rejoined his group of companions, lying down behind a young man with tousled, brown hair. The young man barely noticed Bruno's presence since a young woman had her head buried in his groin. As she ran her tongue the length of his shaft and back again, he curled his hands in her hair and closed his eyes, moaning softly. Bruno wrapped his arms around the young man's chest, kissed him once, lingeringly, on the neck and then slid his cock between the young man's arse cheeks. The man's eyes opened wide with shock, but then closed again, and his moans doubled as the woman at his groin swallowed the whole length of him while Bruno thrust into him from behind.

"What is Rule Five?" Lily asked, tearing her eyes away from the group. She had no desire to join them, yet their cries of pleasure sent spirals of desire curling up her legs and into her darkest places.

"Rule Five," announced Jack, never taking his eyes off the group, "is that your pleasures may make you the person you are, but you must never let them rule you." Lily saw his hand move down to the bulge in his trousers, stroking it lightly, thoughtfully. Such was the faraway look in his eyes that Lily doubted whether he even knew he was doing it.

A sudden compulsion and wildness seized her, and she reached out to slip her hand under his. She felt the long, hard length of him beneath her fingertips, and she ran her hand up and down it once. Jack's eyelids fluttered closed as she stroked him, and she saw a faint smile tug at the corners of his lips. Then his hand closed over hers and held her still. He opened his eyes and looked at her.

"Not quite yet," he said, his voice thick with desire. "We have one more rule yet. Follow me."

The Making of a Queen

The sixth and final square was completely empty except for a large throne in the middle. Jack stopped and looked at Lily expectantly. Lily peered all around the square, even moving to check behind the throne, but the square was deserted except for the pair of them.

"There's no one here," Lily said in disappointment. "How am I to learn the final rule and become Queen Lily?"

Jack's eyes sparkled as he walked toward her. He stopped just a foot away from her, so close that, if Lily had wanted to, she could have reached out and touched him. If she chose, she could have run her hand down his chest, over his toned stomach, and lower to encircle him completely. She wanted to, but she didn't.

"You don't need anyone else for this final lesson," Jack said. "Rule Six: know yourself." There was a pause as Lily looked at him expectantly.

"Is that it?" she asked eventually. Jack moved closer, staring down at Lily. Her throat felt very dry.

"I have shown you the pleasures in which society indulges. There are many other weird and wonderful things in this forest if you care to go looking for them, but before you do, you must know yourself. Know your own desires and your own limits. Out of everything I've shown you, Lily, what is it that you want the most?"

Lily's reply was immediate. "All of it," she whispered.

Jack choked back a laugh. "You want it all?" he said. It was the first time all day he had looked surprised.

"Yes," said Lily indignantly. "It's my prerogative as queen. I want everything, and I shall have it. I want to play games. I want to be a tool for pleasure. I want to be charmed. I want to control and be submissive. I want to indulge my every whim with everyone and anyone, but first of all with you."

"You want quite a lot," remarked Jack.

"You want quite a lot, *Your Majesty*," said Lily with a sly smile.

Jack bowed low. "But of course," he replied in a deep, confident voice. "Then, would Your Majesty care to ascend to her throne?" Lily beamed at the suggestion and made of show of sitting down in a most regal manner. Jack bowed again.

"How grand Your Majesty looks," he observed. Lily thought his tone held a hint of mockery. "All that is lacking is a crown," Jack added. He stepped to the side of the throne and picked up an intricately woven band of gold studded with gems. He moved to stand behind the throne, and Lily couldn't help a small giggle of pleasure escaping her lips. It was all such fun.

"I crown you, Queen Lily," intoned Jack's voice from behind her. A broad grin split Lily's face as she waited, but she could not feel the crown being placed on her head.

It is so delicate and light, she thought, *that perhaps it is sitting there and I simply cannot feel it.*

Lily raised her hands up to determine whether the crown was already sitting on her head, and she felt Jack grab her wrist. She cried out and struggled, but quick as a flash he had tied her to the top of the throne with a thin cord. She tried to reach out with her other hand to unknot it, but Jack swiftly grabbed that one as well and secured it in the same manner on the other side.

Lily squirmed and wriggled but could not twist herself free. As Jack walked sedately back around in front of her, she looked at him in fury.

"You were supposed to crown me," she said angrily. He shook his head, a smile playing over his lips.

"Not quite yet, Lily. I haven't granted your requests yet. I believe you asked to play a game, so that is what we are doing. You wanted to be controlled, so I have tied you so that you may not escape whatever I do to you. You desire me to be charming, so my tongue is at your bidding. You want to be a tool for pleasure, and so, my sweet, you will be. But you also wanted to control and to indulge in your every whim with your subjects. As I am your subject, you must command me."

"Untie me," demanded Lily immediately. Jack looked her up and down with a sly grin.

"No," he said firmly. Lily fell silent.

"Kiss me then," she commanded instead. She felt herself flush at making such a bold demand, but Jack merely raised his eyebrow.

"Where?" he asked.

Lily could feel her blush deepening, but she tried to compensate by looking imperious. "On the lips, to begin with," she said. Jack approached the throne, leaned over her and planted a delicate kiss on her lips. "Again," she murmured. "Deeper this time."

Lily parted her lips as Jack kissed her, and his tongue sought out hers, caressing it. Images flashed through Lily's mind of where she might direct that tongue to next, and then Jack pulled away. He waited expectantly.

"Now, on my neck," she said, turning her head to expose her smooth, white flesh. Jack bent his head, resting his lips against her skin. Lily gasped as he nipped her gently before pulling away. She cleared her throat.

"Now undress," she commanded. Jack stood back and unlaced first his jerkin, then his breeches. When he stood fully naked and erect before her, Lily could not help but stare at his cock. It twitched under her wanton gaze.

"Undress me next," she said, her voice low. Jack reached into his pile of clothes and produced a small knife. He unsheathed it, then deftly cut away the fabric of Lily's dress. She wriggled as her skin was exposed to the air. The wooden throne felt rough beneath her smooth buttocks.

"Excellent," she said. Her imperious tone was spoiled by the quaver of desire within it. "Now," she commanded, "charm me."

"But of course, my queen," said Jack. He gave a low bow but did not rise. Instead, he knelt before Lily and, running his hands up her legs, he eased her thighs apart. Lily sighed in anticipation as his caress reached the top of her legs and his fingers brushed over her curls.

Jack bent his head and kissed first up the inside of one thigh, then the other. He started at her knee and stopped just when she wished he would go on. He repeated this with each leg so that Lily was trembling with frustration when he finally planted a slow deep kiss on her clit.

Lily moaned with delight as his tongue circled and rubbed around the center of her pleasure. Then she gasped as it delved lower and dipped inside her. She wriggled as he continued his slow, teasing kisses. Arousal was racing through her like fire. When Jack moved back to suckle on her tiny mound once more, Lily felt her orgasm begin to build. As it started to crest within her, Lily arched her back and cried out. But before she could go spiraling through the heights of pleasure, Jack pulled away and stood up.

She had been trembling before, but now the whole of Lily's body shook with desperate frustration.

"I command you to finish what you started, Carpenter," she said, furious.

"I will do as you bid, of course," replied Jack with a devious smile. "But not that way. Choose another way, Lily."

Her mind was whirling with lust and need, and Lily could not think of what to ask for. "I don't know," she confessed. "You decide."

Jack raised an eyebrow. "Is that your command—that I decide?" he asked.

Lily nodded. Her hair fell in her eyes, but, with her hands tied, she could not brush it aside.

"Very well," Jack said. He stepped forward and lifted her legs, placing his own legs on either side of the throne. He sat on the throne and, with a wicked smile, he lowered Lily slowly onto him. As Jack's thick member parted her flesh and nuzzled inside her, Lily gave out a gasp. It became a low, guttural moan as she sank farther onto him. She was desperate to throw her arms around him and hold him close, but the bonds prevented her. Instead, she wrapped her legs around his waist, pulling him closer and deeper inside her. She thought Jack might object, but she saw that need burned in his eyes as much as in hers.

Jack's hands moved round to hold Lily's buttocks, and he held her steady as he started to move within her. Lily leaned forward and kissed his neck, grazing it with her teeth just as he had done to hers. She heard a moan escape his lips, and he drove into her harder.

Such was the power behind Jack's thrusts that Lily had to brace herself against the chair. She pressed her back against it, and her fingers found purchase in the intricate carvings at the top of the throne. Her right hand found a rampant wooden lion while her left gripped a prancing unicorn, and so she held herself firm while Jack drove deeper into her than ever before.

Sweat was running down both their bodies, but Jack's rhythm never faltered. He threw every ounce of energy into fucking Lily, his cries matching hers each time he thrust every last inch of himself inside her.

Lily felt her climax building again, and she urged Jack on with cries and moans.

And suddenly she was tumbling through fires of wantonness, every nerve in her body tingling then burning as pleasure shivered through her. Jack bucked underneath her, his climax timed perfectly with her own. As the waves of desire washed through them then gradually subsided, Lily let her body relax and fall against Jack. When their breathing had slowed, he undid her restraints. She put her arms around him, burying her face in his neck.

"Again," she murmured breathlessly. She felt Jack's body shake with laughter beneath her.

"As you command, my queen," he said softly.

Jack obeyed every demand that Lily could invent, his energy and enthusiasm matching her own. Having ridden him hard and fast on the soft moss beneath the throne, Lily demanded that Jack screw her up against the tree. She commanded that he stay still while she tasted every inch of his cock with her tongue, before she drew him down onto her and they rutted on the grass like a pair of beasts. Then Jack wrapped her in his arms and they shuddered their way to a final orgasm as the sky began to darken.

Lily lay in Jack's arms, watching the stars come out of hiding in the heavens above them. She felt warm, sated, and content. Jack wore a smile of satisfaction similar to her own.

"If this is a chessboard," Lily asked, her voice low, "what lies in all the other squares?"

"Many wonders, Lily," Jack replied sleepily, "many more than you can imagine."

Lily considered this. "Then we shall have to explore them together, you and I," she replied. "When your duties of Royal Carpenter allow, of course," she added.

Jack drew her closer to him. "As Your Majesty commands," he murmured into her hair, and they lay like that until dawn began to creep across the sky.

A World of Her Own
Alex Picchetti

She prefers here to the real world.

Oh, the Red Queen has her rages and the White Queen can barely manage her life, but they are so much more vibrant than the people in Alice's life. Her solid husband and her brilliant, insufferable sister seem like paintings in a museum by comparison: pretty enough to look at, but only fit for discussion. Alice prefers to experience life.

And it is an experience. Tonight the Red Queen is holding a feast in her honor and has already threatened four chefs with beheadings. Two more have quit. Alice can only laugh while the King runs scattershot through his palace, trying to calm everyone in his wife's wake.

"It's not necessary," Alice tries to reassure her, but the Red Queen will have none of it.

"You're as bad as the other one," she grumps. "If you just let things be, nothing gets done. *I wanted blue!*" she screams out a window at the card-men. "My dear, are those spades or clubs? Oh, pay it no mind. I'll have all their heads."

"Of course you will," Alice tells her soothingly. "Now come back to bed."

"I have far too many things to do, my girl," her lover says crossly. "Go visit the other one. She'll have nothing better to do, I'm sure." And with that she flounces away.

Alice considers for a moment the red ribbons tying her in place. Her arms are bound against the headboard in beautiful crisscross pattern, but one that she can't seem to wriggle free of. "A tart pattern for a little tart," the Queen had said affectionately.

It is the Cheshire cat who finds her first. She doesn't remember when he began his transformation in this world, but now he is more man than cat; when she came of age, he was practically a panther. "He had a voice like wild honey and skin as soft as down..." That made her wonder if Mr. Kipling had a Wonderland of his own in India. Now, only the brilliant smile that appears first and vanishes last and his long tail remind her of what he was once.

"You seem to have a predicament," his smile says.

"Well." She glances at the ribbons and gives them an experimental tug. "My arms *are* growing tired." She shifts her hips, sliding against the sheets the Queen so carelessly left resting against her mound and sighs happily. "I can't say it's *all* bad, though—no, not all."

"I doubt this was intentional," he says, twitching the sheets away with a slowly appearing hand. She pouts at the space that will be his eyes. "Do you think she meant to leave you like this?"

"Trussed like a Christmas goose for you?" she asks saucily.

37

The rest of the arm appears, and he caresses up the inside of her thigh. "I thought the feast was for you, not featuring you." There are his eyes, crinkled with laugh lines.

"I don't think she shares well."

"And yet here you are..." The remainder of his face appears at her breast suddenly, and she gasps and giggles as he licks her nipple with his raspy, dry tongue. "A perfect little toy."

"Stop that," she says, trying to be stern, but she is arching her back in time with his licking, trying to gain purchase against his leg—which she can see he is hiding from her. "You are terrible!"

"I must think the Queen meant to do this. I will have to thank her later." He traces his tongue up the side of her neck and laps at her earlobe.

"Oh, do stop, that tickles!"

His tail begins its slow trail up her body until the tip flicks against her face like a powder brush. "Did you ever do this to your poor kitten? Tickle her nose with her tail? I must use this opportunity to make you suffer such indignity. *Quid pro quo*, or perhaps *caveat emptor*, as the Latin says." The tail slides down the other side of her neck to flick rapidly across her swollen nipples.

"Oh!" She struggles in vain against the bonds. "You are the worst creature in all of Wonderland! If I were free, you would do as I say." She hooks her leg around his waist and pulls him to her, trapping him in place against her.

He laughs and holds her hips firmly, preventing her from rubbing against his cock as she wants desperately to do. "Ah, Alice. Has any cat anywhere been truly trapped?"

"I used to grab Dinah and kiss her—like so." She drops soft little kisses along his cheeks and gives one large one right on the tip of his nose.

"Dinah endured those because she loved you," he tells her solemnly. "If she had liked you less, she would have done this." And he vanishes and reappears outside her grasp, pushing her legs together so that she can't try that trick again. "Or, perhaps this." With his free hand, he traces one sharp claw against her cheek and down her throat. "You see, we are fickle creatures. Nothing we do is for *your* benefit."

"I can see that," she says crossly. His claw bites a little more deeply and she takes a sharp breath. "But there must be something we can do that we will both enjoy?" she asks more demurely.

He smiles. "That would be for your benefit." He stands, running his fingers through her hair. His cock is erect before her, and he pulls her to it.

Alice knows this game; they have played it before, far more interesting than chess (of which she never did grasp the intricacies, much to her sister's annoyance) and much more difficult to win. She would try to bring him to climax as quickly as possible while he used his fingers and his tail to drive her quite mad. Begging meant losing, and currently her opponent was in the lead.

Her tongue slips around the head of his dick, lapping at his come. She smiles inwardly. He has excited himself too much already. She moans as the tip of his tail brushes—so lightly—against her vulva. *Don't be arrogant*, she scolds herself. She tightens her lips around his shaft and begins working his cock in earnest.

The Cheshire cat tightens his fingers in her hair appreciatively, slowing her pace ever so slightly. He admires the artistic interplay between the lightness of her hair and skin and his own. *Who knew that such a precocious little girl would grow up into this succubus?* he thinks. His tail, almost of its own accord, dances across her inner thighs, and he chuckles as she twitches and moans, still fighting futilely against the ribbons that hold her in place so perfectly. The vibrations of her lips seem to reverberate up his spine and down into his balls, muscles rippling in ecstasy. *When did she become so good at this?*

She wants desperately to grip his ass, feel the clenching beneath her fingers, massage his opening for the satisfying sound of his surprise and enjoyment. She is going to find a way to capture him, she vows, and make him suffer the same torment he is putting her through.

She pulls away from his cock to blow cool air on the wet surface, then begins to trace intricate patterns down his shaft with her hot tongue. They gaze at each other, each trying to intimidate the other into losing the game. Straining against her bonds to reach, she finally uses the very tip of her tongue to caress the spot between the end of his dick and the soft skin of his balls. The downy hair tickles her tongue, but he grunts, his cock twitching hard against her cheek, and he spills his seed.

The intensity of it brings him to his knees between her legs, and she gives him a smug, satisfied grin. He laughs, kissing and biting at her lips. "You have been practicing."

"A lady never reveals her secrets," she says primly.

"And now something for you," he says, bending between her spread legs. Alice nearly cries in relief. Finally it is her turn—

"Oh!" she yelps as his claws dig into her thigh. "What was that for?"

"Marking," he says cheerfully. He twists her skin and shows her the red welts that say *CC*. "After all, you may be a Queen, but I am a cat." He kisses the cuts, suckling at them and running his tongue against them gently, enjoying Alice's soft gasps. "And no matter how grand you may be, a cat may look at a Queen—and much more besides." He kisses her deeply then, and sharply rakes his claws down the ribbons that bind her.

She tries to grab him with her freed arms, but he vanishes save for his smile and his cock, which wiggles at her mockingly before vanishing entirely.

She scowls deeply at the space he had occupied. Just like him to amuse himself at her expense. She pulls off the ribbon remains and stretches her arms, then massages her hands to rid them of the tingling sensations. She goes to the Red Queen's vanity, trying to control the quite unladylike sexual frustration and rage flowing through her veins.

"How dare he?" she asks her reflection as she begins to tear a brush through her hair. "And just look at how he has left my hair."

Her reflection shrugs. "It could be worse," she

says with a hint of jealousy. "You could be here, with..." She glances behind her, where Alice can hear Rolf cursing at his cuffs. "At least *he*—" her reflection means the Cheshire Cat— "has some imagination."

"Oh, my dear," says Alice. "I know you understand!"

"Someday you will come back, won't you?" says her reflection plaintively. "Honestly, your sister just fawns over Rolf—it makes me ill to watch. How anyone could want that, I can't even imagine, and you know I can imagine quite a lot!" Alice nods appreciatively. "Everything is so *boring* here all the time. Why, we saw an opera the other night and everyone died. And not one orgasm to make it worthwhile! It was dreadful."

"I will come back, someday," says Alice. "Just bear it a little longer. I need to strengthen my constitution for it."

"Alice, are you talking to yourself again?" her husband asks. "I have told you not to do that. You get more than enough conversation gossiping with the neighbors; do you need to hear yourself quite so much?"

Her reflection smiles at her husband, and it is only because it is Alice's own face that she recognizes the hardness behind it. "I'll be right there, dearest," she trills. When he has left, her reflection turns back to Alice. "Do be quick," she begs.

Alice nods. "I won't leave you there for too long." She kisses the mirror. "It is a shame we can't both be on this side."

"Oh, that would be fun!"

Alice shares a sly smile with her mirror-world self, but Rolf calls again and her reflection leaves. The anger flares in her again. *Men*, she thinks derisively. She summons one of the card-men to her room to dress her. She revenges herself on the Cheshire Cat by flirting shamelessly with the servant, asking him to assist her with her underthings and her corset, giving him long looks at her legs as he pushes the stockings up them, and shifting her hips so as to brush against his hands and legs as he laces her corset and prepares her petticoats. She wonders if he can smell her arousal. It is cruel of her, but his flustered expression makes her laugh so!

"Fetch me a dress," she demands. "Something with an abundance of lace. I will be visiting the White Queen."

He bows and scrapes his way out of the bedroom, and she can hear him fleeing.

"Oh, I am terrible, aren't I?" she asks the empty room. "I shall have to try to be better. Not good... just better!"

He returns with another of the cards, together carrying her calling toilette—a vision in a dazzling shade of blue. She examines it critically, complaining of the leg-o'mutton sleeves, but what can one do in the face of fashion? She sends them away with an annoyed flick of her wrist, then goes to the balcony.

And up, and over the ledge and she is away, flying to the ground and across it, over the river and past the train, waving daintily to the passengers as royalty must, and then up again onto the balcony of the Red Queen's greatest rival and dearest friend.

The White Queen is blowing delicate patterns of colored smoke out into the air, taking sips from the gargantuan hookah at her side. As Alice lands, the Queen gives her a woozy smile and puffs a smoky red heart around her face.

"The Caterpillar brought me some very... interesting gifts," she informs Alice. "The petit fours are on the chest of drawers..."

Alice slides a hand around the Queen's tiny waist. "I'm afraid I didn't come for a social visit," she whispers into her ear. Her mind is full of the smoke, and it is driving her passions mad. Her wrath at the Cheshire cat returns in full force, together with her need to fuck.

She backs her partner against the hookah, glad of its size and sturdiness. She pins the Queen and kisses her deeply, driving their bodies together. Suddenly the wealth of petticoats between the two of them seems aggravating rather than enticing. Her fingers wind through the platinum strands of her lover's hair, trailing down to the closures of the dress.

"Alice!" gasps the Queen. "You're being quite forward!" She looks like a doll, two perfect pink circles on alabaster skin. "What if someone sees?"

"Then they will wish that they could be Queen," Alice says impatiently. She twirls the smaller woman deftly, pressing her against the smooth glass curve with the weight of her body. "Now do be quiet, these buttons are maddening." In fact, she decides, they are too difficult to deal with, and she instead begins to lift the layers upon layers of silk that hide her prize from her.

The Queen is wearing no underthings, and her bottom is delightfully red. She squirms as Alice runs her fingers along the curve of one cheek. "What is this from?" Alice asks in her ear. She twists the fabric in one hand and presses it into the small of the monarch's back.

The Queen's blush deepens. "The King grew bored of counting his money," she says.

"Oh?" Alice begins to stroke one finger against her pussy.

"Ah!" She rocks back against the touch. "And so he decided... to count strokes." Her breath is coming in tiny gasps.

The red blush is so pretty against her skin that Alice dips her head to the curve of her neck and bites. She works a second finger into the Queen's cunt, rubbing her thumb on the slick skin between her folds. She wants to consume this woman totally. "And where is he now?"

"Asleep in bed," sighs the Queen. "He is quite easy to please." She begins to shudder and grind herself against the elegant green glass of the hookah, then cries out several times and jerks sharply.

"He's not the only one," Alice laughs. She kisses the butterfly-shaped marks on the Queen's neck as she brings her fingers up for the woman to suckle at eagerly. "Now come with me."

The Queen takes another puff on the hookah before following Alice obediently into the bedroom. Sure enough, the King is draped over the pillows, snoring loudly, his cock twitching occasionally.

Alice pushes the Queen back onto the bed. "I

have had enough of men today," she says conversationally, removing her drawers. "I have *not* had enough pleasure."

"Something must be done," her lover says, fluttering her eyelashes coquettishly.

"Indeed," Alice says and drapes her skirts over the pale woman's face, kneeling. The Queen understands her immediately and begins to explore Alice's entrance with her tongue.

The girl lifts her petticoats briefly to regard her partner. "I would hate you to think I am not enjoying this," she whispers. "But I must be very quiet, so as not to wake your husband."

The Queen mumbles in agreement, and Alice lets the layers of lace and muslin drop back into place. The pipe slithers up beside her on the bed, as though alive—*It is Wonderland*, she thinks, *it may be*—and she begins to suck at it, considering the sleeping King before her.

Unlike his counterpart, he is quite large. In most ways. The expanse of his chest is covered in curls of platinum hair. She wonders what it would be like to grip it, tug it gently as he fucks her...

Alice sighs softly as the Queen sucks on one of her nether lips, then the other. She squeals in surprise as a finger works its way into her anus, green smoke erupting from her mouth. She looks quickly to see if they will be caught, but the King does not wake.

"You are a demon!" she hisses at the Queen, and the pair erupt into helpless giggles, the Queen's breath bursting against Alice's pussy in a quite pleasant way. Alice begins to rub against her more insistently, focusing all of her attention on the pressure building within her cunt. The Queen slips a finger inside her, then another; slowly she continues until she has her whole hand inside Alice. She flickers her tongue rapidly over Alice's clit, trying her very best to make her cry out.

But Alice will not make a sound—her pride depends on it, now. Even her slow rocking may wake the King. But oh, God, if she doesn't want to thrash madly against that hand, those lips... She rocks faster and faster.

The King snorts and rolls over, and she gasps, the thrill of being caught bringing her to the cusp. She thrashes there for a long moment until the Queen's tongue runs down the inside of her thigh, catching against the Cheshire cat's mark. With a wail Alice crashes into her orgasm, all thought of silence left behind in the wake of this wave of intense ecstasy.

Still the King sleeps!

Alice crawls off the Queen, legs like rubber. Her lover's face and fingers are sticky and wet, and Alice begins to giggle madly. The Queen pouts at her with mock crossness.

"I SAY!" bellows the King, sitting up suddenly. "IS IT ME, OR IS IT QUITE HOT IN HERE?"

The women shriek and flee to the balcony to hide the evidence of their indiscretions. Alice begins to wipe at her lover's face as the Queen calls back inside, "No, my love, it is quite warm—*ouch, Alice, that hurts*—Such a lovely summer's day!"

"IS THAT ALICE?" he asks.

"I came to tell you that the Red Queen is having a

feast," Alice says, scrubbing rapidly. Well, it *is* true, for a given definition of true. "I was just leaving."

"JOLLY GOOD," he says, and they hear him roll over and begin snoring again.

"And where are you going to?" a voice floats up from the courtyard.

As one, she and the Queen peer over the railing. The White Knight waves up at them. He has tied himself to his horse so as not to fall but still seems to be canting to one side.

"Back to the Red Queen's castle," Alice says.

"I expect *you* could go quite quickly," he says glumly.

"Oh, I can, but" she says, seeing his sad face, "I would prefer the company."

He perks up at that. "Well, then! I shall be the one to take you!"

The White Queen kisses Alice on tippytoe. "Don't forget to write," she calls as Alice jumps down to land gracefully in the saddle.

"She shall see me in a few hours. Whatever would I write to her?" Alice says to the Knight as they canter off.

He smiles. "You can tell her of our adventures."

Their trip takes more time than Alice would take on her own, but it is a pleasant way to spend the afternoon, visiting old friends and passing by old haunts. She leans against the Knight as though he is a comfortable seat that travels the countryside, tugging at his curls every so often to amuse herself with their bounce.

They pass by a dark wood that she does not recognize. The Knight seems preoccupied by it, and

48

finally she becomes so curious that she must know. "Who lives there?"

"The sisters," he tells her. "The Jub-Jub Bird, the Bandersnatch, and the Jabberwocky."

"I thought the Jabberwocky had been killed," she says with a yawn. "Isn't that how the story goes?"

He shakes his head. "She is immortal, I think. And when you are immortal..." He shakes his head. "You can become very creative."

That piques her interest, but he refuses to tell her more, except to say that he has seen them, but only once, and that was enough for some time, thank you, and that "nice young women shouldn't go to such places."

"You think I am a nice young woman?" she asks.

He wraps an arm around her waist. "I do."

They finish their ride in companionable silence, the horse unperturbed from his winding route.

When they arrive back at the castle, the party is already in full swing, wine flowing freely and the guests in the midst of some interesting variation on a parlor game. The Red King is stroking his hands along the curve of the White Queen's body, who in turn is massaging the buttocks of a soused Mad Hatter, who is nuzzling against the Duchess, all of them in varying states of undress.

The White Knight hastily excuses himself, and Alice has no time to stop him, for the Duchess gloms on to her immediately and begins to caress her breasts.

"Do as I do," she mumbles into Alice's ear.

She is so amazed by the scene before her that she does not move, and it is not until Tweedledee—or is

Tweedledum? Even after all these years she cannot tell the difference—shouts "A FORFEIT!" that she realizes she has lost the game, and the motley group descends on her to remove her dress.

After that, the commands grow more and more licentious until the Hatter, pantsless, is kneeling before the White Queen, who is sitting atop the Red Queen's throne, furiously licking her clit as the White King licks the shaft of *his* prick, and when he, panting, calls to Alice, "Do as I do," she is more than happy to thrust herself on his cock. Oh, it is even better than she had imagined!

She glimpses the Cheshire cat in the rafters, and he waves saucily at her, his other hand stroking his dick languorously. She sticks her tongue out at him, and he wags his dick at her, as if to remind her of the morning's events. She glares at him, but he remains smug.

Returning her attention to the game, she beckons the twins to her and commands them to do as she does. As though of one mind, they each turn to one of her pert pink nipples and begin to suckle at them. They still have a boyish innocence to them, their ears too big, their noses still freckled; but they have mastered this art, and she rewards them with her moans, running her fingers through their hair.

The Red Queen slides up behind them, taking one cock in each hand and stroking the heads against Alice's thighs. "I shall do as you are doing," she says, and although it is not a question, they nod, tugging Alice's breasts pleasantly.

The Red Queen and Alice regard each other for a few moments. "Didn't I have you tied up?" the monarch says finally.

"You did, Your Majesty."

"I will have to punish you for escaping," she says thoughtfully.

"With all due respect, Your Majesty, it was the Cat's fault." She shifts her position on the King's cock, groaning happily at the new stimulation.

"Be that as it may, you were the disobedient one." The Queen squeezes the twins' cocks in tandem, whispering directions in their ears. They begin to bite and nibble at the undersides of Alice's breasts as the Queen takes Alice's head in her hands, stroking her scalp with her fingernails and running her fingers through her hair. Alice shivers as the Queen begins to kiss her slowly, stretching over Tweedledee and Tweedledum. Everyone around them is frantic, manic; but the Red Queen will not be rushed. She kisses Alice deeply.

Alice thrills at it. She can't help but wonder if there is some ulterior motive to it all. The Queen has always been able to twist her mind, and it excites her immensely.

The Queen parts from her, still close enough to feel the movement of her eyelashes and lips. "This is a silly game," she says quietly. "Who do you truly obey?"

"You, Your Majesty," Alice says demurely.

"Louder, girl."

"You, Your Majesty." Her cunt clenches against the White King's cock.

"Take pride in it!"

"YOU, YOUR MAJESTY!"

Her orgasm sends a shock through the whole party,

and in the haze of pleasure she thinks she hears rocks falling in the distance and a clanking noise. She clings to the shoulders of Tweedledee and Tweedledum as she rocks herself madly against the King, a new orgasm chasing on the heels of each old one. When she finally, trembling, pulls herself out of the orgy, the Red Queen abruptly stands and claps her hands.

"Dinner shall begin as soon as everyone is dressed," she announces, adding, "and I am *very* famished." Recognizing a threat when they hear it, the guests scramble to find their clothes and rush for the dinner table, save for the White King, who has fallen asleep again.

Alice, dizzy from the intensity, is the last to find her heap of clothing. As she picks it up, she sees on the wall a mirror, and her reflection gazing at her.

"Oh, my dear," she says, approaching. "Were you watching all that?"

Her reflection nods. "It isn't good of me to be envious of you, but you do have all the fun."

Alice smiles, a little ruefully. "You have been very patient with me." She kisses the mirror. "I am sure the Queen has some ideas in her head for me—or for *you*, as it may be."

Her reflection perks up immediately. "I would like that."

"So would I," says Alice, as she begins to push through the mirror—does she imagine that brush of fur against her cheek?

—and through again to the real world.

It takes her a moment to gain her bearing again; even after twenty years of it, she still has trouble with the return home. *Perhaps*, she thinks, *it is because* here *is not so nearly as nice as* there. She is in the parlor, it is evening, and out of the corner of her eye, her reflection waves in the mirror and scampers off.

"Really, Alice," her husband is saying, "some days I don't think you listen to me at all. Always with your head in the clouds!"

"I am sorry," she says. "I suppose I must be more tired than I thought."

He shakes his head. "Well, off to bed then," he says crossly. "I will see your family out."

"Thank you, darling," she says, giving him a kiss on the cheek.

And as she drifts off to sleep, she rubs her legs together and sighs happily, and hopes she dreams about the other Alice's adventures.

Tarts and Tea
Holly Abair

"Do you hear me, Alice? This nonsense needs to stop!" Her sister's fingers dug into her shoulders so tightly that she knew she would be bruised in the morning. The sapphire eyes that stared into her own were filled with a mixture of determination, anger, and a hint of underlying fear.

Alice did not respond at first, her gaze breaking away from Susan's to stare at the kerosene lamp that softly flickered on the bedside table. It had been five years since her first journey down the rabbit hole. It was as if Wonderland had become a part of her, a part that she couldn't put into her past. "They weren't just dreams, Susan. It was real."

Susan shook her sister, her voice a low hiss. "I am getting married, Alice! I won't be here to protect you any longer. Mum was saying today that she was going to see the doctors at Cane Hill. They're going to stick you in a madhouse! You're thirteen now, and these... these... delusions scare her!"

After a long moment of silence, Susan's grip on her shoulders relaxed slightly. "Promise me, Alice! Promise that you will never speak of this again!"

Alice met her sister's wide, fearful eyes again. Susan looked to be on the verge of tears. "I promise, Susan. No more talk of Wonderland."

Susan nodded, releasing her shoulders. Alice slipped beneath the thick down comforter, turning to face the wall. She clutched her stuffed cat to her chest, the toy that reminded her so much of Cheshire. The room darkened as Susan put out the lamp.

Alice stared at the shadows dancing across the walls, her mind roaming. She had sworn not to speak of Wonderland, but she was determined to find it again. She wouldn't tell anyone, but she still believed.

* * *

Eight years later

Alice woke abruptly, a gasp leaving her throat. She was sitting upright, her heavy breathing filling the dark room. Alice knew from experience that if she closed her eyes she would still see the long table set for tea, the Hatter in one of his vividly colored suits, and the Dormouse snoring in his empty teapot. She could still taste the sweet bitterness of the Hatter's tea on her lips. Strangely, the March Hare had been missing from this dream.

She stood shakily and turned the knob on the wall, watching the newly installed gas lighting flicker to life. Her gaze fell upon the dress that was draped on a frame in the center of the room. Beside it was a basket of pins, needles, thread, and scissors: remnants from her final fitting.

A mild shudder passed through her as she walked

over to it, fingers brushing gently over the ivory lace and delicate embroidery. Her father had finally found her a suitable match, despite the "oddness" that had occurred during her childhood. It had been years since Alice had dreamed of Wonderland. She tried shaking it off as prewedding jitters.

She crossed the room and turned down the gas knob, determined to get a bit more rest. In the morning, she would be a married woman, living far from her childhood home. It was her last night in this room, with all of its beautiful nightmares. Her eyes widened at that thought. This was her last chance to get back to Wonderland.

One last look, she promised herself, *and then I will be through with this childish nonsense.*

Shaking her head at her own insanity, Alice buckled on her ankle-length boots. She rose, clad only in her thin cotton nightdress, and crept silently from her room. Alice tiptoed down the stairs and out of the kitchen door. Once she had passed the point that anyone could hear her, Alice broke into an unladylike run.

Alice moved from the path, into the meadow beyond. The grasses were blanketed with dew. It soaked her legs up to midthigh, plastering her gown to her body. She reached the ancient tree at the edge of the meadow and sank to the ground at its base. The tree itself had withered and died, a dark skeleton with limbs that twisted into the night sky. The rabbit hole remained, half-collapsed at the base of the trunk. Alice settled herself as comfortably as she could in the cool grass, shivering as it soaked her nightdress further. She focused on the rabbit hole and began her vigil.

* * *

Alice sat up with a yawn, her hand brushing a strand of her corn-silk hair from her face. The sun was edging closer to the horizon but had not yet risen, lightening the sky from nearly black to a cobalt blue. She rose from the ground, grateful that no one was around to see the state of her clothing. The damp grasses had soaked through the nightdress, causing it to cling revealingly to her body. Her chilled nipples pressed visibly against the fabric. A shiver passed through her, and she wished that she had thought to bring a coat.

Alice stretched, trying to relieve the stiffness in her neck and shoulders. She berated herself for her foolishness. Instead of sleeping on her soft down mattress, she had spent the night on the hard, cold ground. She shook her head, blaming her rash behavior on the upcoming wedding.

"Come, Alice, you've put all this behind you." She tried to keep the disappointed edge from her voice. "After all if there were anything to find at this silly old rabbit hole, wouldn't you have found it by now?"

Alice gave the hole a mournful glance and turned to walk away. She knew that she would have to make haste to be back before anyone would be up to notice her absence. Bitter disappointment filled her. Was her family right? Was she truly mad?

"So escaping with your head attached once was not enough for you, Alice. You want another go at the madhouse."

Alice froze, the familiar voice sending a tingle

down her spine. Taking a deep breath, she spun around. A disembodied grin and a pair of golden eyes floated above one of the bare limbs of the tree.

"I need the truth, Cat. Besides"—tears sprang to her eyes, and the next words left her in a barely audible whisper—"I don't belong here."

"Oh, Alice..." the feline's voice was tinged with an odd note of sympathy, "I thought that you didn't want to go among mad people."

Alice smiled, the bitter note in her voice surprising her. "But they're all mad here."

The grin faded from view, and the figure of a man began to appear at the base of the tree. First his head appeared. Mahogany hair framed a masculine, angular face. Luminous, golden cat eyes stared at her hungrily, sending a chill through her. The huge grin of the cat relaxed into a rakish smile, revealing elongated canine teeth.

Alice took a deep breath, tearing herself away from his gaze to take in the rest of him. The man was tall and slender, yet muscular, though built more for stealth and speed than brute strength. He wore a scarlet pinstripe jacket that looked like it would be soft if she dared to get close enough to touch it. Dark pants molded snugly to his thighs before vanishing into knee-length boots. Her eyes met his again, causing her breath to catch in her throat. The look in their amber depths left no doubts as to which of them was the predator and which was the prey.

She opened her mouth to speak, but only a small squeak escaped her. She took a deep breath and tried again. "Cat? Y-You're human?"

"In a manner of speaking, my dear. You may return with me, if you wish, but you will find Wonderland different from what it was on your first journey." His laughter was a rich sound that seemed to coat all of her senses. His eyes raked her frame from head to toe, a grin spreading across his face. "Of course, if you play your cards right, you'll find it much more than you bargained for."

He held out his hand, the amused glint in his eyes almost daring her to take it. "Well?"

Taking a deep breath, Alice moved toward him. The few feet that lay between them seemed to take an eternity for her to cross, her heart pounding with each step. She reached out a delicate hand and placed it against his open palm. His hand closed around hers in a steely grip, not hurting her, but letting her feel his potential strength. Arousal coursed through her veins, tainted by the smallest touch of fear.

He leaned toward her, inhaling deeply, his grin spreading to rival that of his other form. "You smell better than I imagined you would."

Cat's other hand reached up and gently caressed the side of her face. A sigh slipped from her throat as she pressed her face against it, craving the touch. His other hand released hers, his arm snaking around her waist, pulling her body closer to his. He brushed a strand of hair from her face and then gently threaded his fingers through her hair. A soft whimper escaped her as he leaned his face closer to hers, his predatory eyes gleaming in the light of the setting moon.

He pressed his lips against hers with surprising softness. Then his fist tightened in her hair as he kissed her with increasing intensity. Alice's lips parted, and his tongue plundered her mouth possessively. She melted into the kiss, her knees buckling. All that held her upright was his arm wrapped firmly around her waist.

When he finally broke away, a faint mewl of protest left her throat. His hand released her hair, though his arm around her waist still kept her upright. She was flushed and breathing heavily, the unexpected lust still assailing her.

"Oh my..." She tried to come up with a witty comment and found herself unable to think.

He gave her a shrug and a grin, his golden eyes filling with mirth. "When you're born a tiger, why act tame?"

Her hands slid down the front of his soft jacket, feeling the muscle that that lay beneath the cloth. She licked her swollen lips, her body aching for more. Alice smiled weakly, all thoughts of her wedding and fiancé forgotten. "What are we waiting for?"

He pulled her even closer. She laid her cheek against the plush jacket, her arms tentatively encircling him. Suddenly, the world surrounding her blurred into shades of gray. Alice tried lifting her head away from his chest to see more, but his hand slid to the back of her head, firmly pressing her to his chest.

"Hold on to me." His voice sounded distant and echoed around her, as if they were standing in a vast, empty space. Then the world went black.

Alice felt a scream building as she plunged into icy nothingness. The only thing keeping her from complete panic was the feel of Cat's arms wrapped securely around her body and his muscular form pressed tightly to her. The fact that she could still feel him gave her a bit of relief as she stood in the unrelenting darkness. She had no idea how much time they spent in the void. Seconds, days, hours—all seemed to blur together as she clung to her invisible protector. Eventually the world turned back to muted shadows. Finally, just as Alice began to think that she could not stand another second of grays, color popped into the world in an instant. She had to squeeze her eyes shut at the sudden invasion of brightness.

She opened her eyes as Cat stepped away from her, brushing nonexistent cobwebs from his jacket. The color of his jacket had changed. Instead of the brilliant scarlet, it was now stripes of storm-cloud and pearly gray. "I *hate* Fading between realms..."

"Why the change?" Alice gestured to the new jacket. "The scarlet was lovely."

"Ah, but her Royal Highness is the only one allowed to wear that color." He smiled a very unpleasant smile, his voice filled with obvious contempt. "Bringing yourself to her attention is most unwise, especially for something so petty as a coat."

Alice heard a loud snoring echoing from above her. She glanced upward and saw that they were in the garden of living flowers. "Why are we here, Cat?"

"I need to speak with a friend." With that, he spun and strode quickly down the path.

Cat walked slightly ahead of her through the forest of flowers, his gait smooth and confident. It was the middle of the night. Alice glanced upward, but the sentient plants were asleep, their petals tightly closed against the chill of the night air.

Her eyes flicked back to her guide, her gaze hungrily devouring his lithe form. His kiss had left her aching for more. Her nipples were hard, pressing against the thin fabric covering them. Though Alice had never possessed a lurid imagination, she could envision him tearing away her clothing and quenching the fire that was burning beneath her skin. Moisture built between her thighs at the thought of his wicked touch.

As if he could hear her thoughts, he was suddenly in front of her, deftly pinning her to a stalk as thick as a large tree. A small noise escaped her as her body began to ache and throb at the thought of him taking her. Her heart pounded from the excitement.

"Oh my poor Alice, I left you wanting. I shall have to be certain to avoid that in the future." The grin faded from sight as he leaned in and grazed his fangs against her bare throat. A whimper escaped her, her hands sliding around his waist and slipping beneath the material of his shirt.

Alice was practically panting as his fingers cupped her breast and gently stroked across the sensitive flesh of her beaded nipple. He gently rolled it between his fingers, causing her breath to catch in her throat. He continued licking and biting along the smooth line from her neck to shoulder, the ache within her becoming unbearable.

She felt a blush burn across her cheeks as his hands moved to her hips, deftly sliding the material covering her legs upward. The last vestiges of propriety left her as he lightly slid his fingers across the slick flesh between her thighs. Cat covered her mouth with his own as his thumb circled the sensitive nub, one of his fingers poised at her entrance.

"Mary Ann!"

Cat's fingers left her as Alice whipped her head toward the sound of the voice, self-consciously tugging her dress back down. The White Rabbit was bounding toward them, an enraged look on his face. Mortified, she buried her face against Cat's jacket.

"Mary Ann! What exactly are you—?" The Rabbit stopped as he realized that it was the Cat. The anger abruptly left his tone. "L-Lord Donovan! I didn't realize that you desired my maid! I would have given her to you long ago."

Alice peeked upward to look at the Cat. He grinned at the Rabbit. "Do not fret, my dear friend. No harm done. Besides, this is not your Mary Ann."

"Alice?" The Rabbit hopped closer, and Alice forced herself to step away from the solid warmth of the feline's chest. He pulled a pair of spectacles from his breast pocket, peering at her through them. After a moment he glanced at the Cat. "You know I can never tell these human women apart."

"Indeed, Briar. You would mistake the Queen herself for your Mary Ann were it not for her elaborate dress."

"The Queen?" Alice looked at him, curiosity getting the better of her embarrassment. "The Queen is human?"

Donovan laughed, the gleam of his canines reminding her that he was not tame. "Surely you did not think that you were the first girl to stumble down a rabbit hole?"

She stared at him for a long moment, unsure of how to respond. She *had* thought herself to be the only one.

"Everything is set for tomorrow evening, milord, as you requested." Briar pulled the golden pocket watch from his waistcoat and stared at it for a long moment. The rabbit turned and hopped down the path with a wave over his shoulder. "Oh dear, I mustn't be late! I am off to Court."

Alice looked up at the feline, a grin spreading across her lips. "Donovan?"

His grin matched her own. "I may be a Cheshire cat, but did you ever wonder about my name?"

"You know, I suppose that I hadn't thought about it. It's been so long since I first met you all." Curiosity burned through her. "The Queen is human? And what did the Rabbit, Briar I suppose, mean when he said that 'Everything is set'? What is happening tomorrow night?"

"Nothing for you to worry about, dear Alice." Donovan put an arm around her, guiding her off the path and up the sloping bank. He led her deeper into the thicket of flowers, the sweet scents of iris and hibiscus tickling her nostrils.

His voice was gently teasing. "Now that we won't be interrupted..."

His lips pressed gently to her own, and his fingers went to the buttons of her nightdress. As he explored her mouth, he deftly undid the first three, spilling her breasts into the cool night air. His hands cupped them, gently massaging, rolling her nipples between his calloused fingers. Alice's eyes closed as she began to ache anew.

One of his hands left her breast and moved to unbutton the rest of her nightdress. He paused from gently pleasuring her aching breasts, sliding his hands up to her shoulders to push the nightdress off them. The soft material fell in a white cloud around her ankles. Alice did not have the chance to be embarrassed by her nudity as his lips left hers and found one of her nipples, closing on the sensitive peak. His fingers found the juncture of her thighs again, stroking her for a moment before one of them slid into her slick passage.

Donovan's thumb found the nub again and caressed it softly as he added a second finger, stretching her tight walls. His fingers thrust within her as he gently tugged her nipple with his teeth. She felt a sudden sharp pain as his fingers thrust through her maidenhead, and then the pleasure overwhelmed her again. Whimpers and moans filled the night air as he skillfully worked her body. Just as she felt that the pleasure was unbearable, he stilled his fingers, sliding them out of her.

Alice opened her eyes, a protest dying on her lips. Donovan stood before her, nude. He was as muscular and graceful as she had imagined. The lightest dusting of hair lay across his defined chest and in a thin line down the center of his body. Her eyes followed its path, a blush rising to her cheeks. His member was thick and long, hard enough to form a bead of moisture at its tip. She knew a bit about the act itself, gleaned from conversations with Susan about her upcoming wedding night, but she had no idea how it could possibly fit.

His fingers gently lifted her chin until she looked at his face. Donovan's smile was reassuring. "Would you like to stop?"

Alice shook her head slowly, and he smiled at her. Wordlessly, he guided her to the ground. She lay on the soft moss, staring up at the quickly lightening sky. Donovan leaned over her and gently kissed her. This time, Alice deepened the kiss, running her tongue along the tip of one of his fangs. He positioned himself at her entrance and gently slid the tip of his cock into her.

Her breath caught in a hiss, her eyes never leaving his glowing, golden ones. He thrust slowly, pushing his way inside her. Alice whimpered as he eased himself in, his restraint clearly showing on his face. When he was fully inside her, he stilled, gently stroking her golden hair.

"Are you all right?"

Such a simple question, yet one to which she herself had no answer. Her mind was reeling, her body aching and yet feeling wonderful all at once. She nodded up at him, not trusting her voice.

Donovan smiled and gently withdrew, thrusting in again slowly. Alice cried out as the sensation sizzled across every nerve she possessed, and he chuckled softly. He kept thrusting, gently and slowly at first, but soon building a faster rhythm as her body adjusted. Alice's hips rose in time with his, her breath coming in pants and leaving in moans. Suddenly, when she thought that the pleasure could not get more intense, his fingers grazed her sensitive nub, and the world around her exploded into a rush of sensation.

She felt a liquid warmth as his orgasm joined her own, his seed spilling from his body.

He rested his head on her chest for a moment, trying to catch his breath. Then Donovan withdrew from her body and rolled to the side, gently shifting her so that her head lay on his chest. "Are you all right, Alice?"

"Yes." The conviction in her own voice surprised herself. "I don't believe that I have been this good for a long time."

"Who is he?" His fingers found her left hand and toyed with the ring that lay upon her finger. There was no note of accusation in his voice, merely mild curiosity.

Alice removed it, barely giving the diamond a glance. She sat up and tossed the ring as far as she could, watching it glint in the morning light as it flew deeper into the flowers. Alice lay back against his chest, curling up against him for warmth. "He's no one. I meant what I said. I have no desire to go back."

As she drifted off to sleep, she heard him mutter under his breath, "I hope that doesn't change."

* * *

Alice woke in a patch of warm sunlight. She stretched, her eyes still closed, skin drinking in the warmth. Then her eyes snapped open as the events of the previous night flooded back into her mind. Alice was still in the clearing, stretched out on a bed of soft, green moss. She noticed that Donovan was nowhere to be seen and was about to call out to him when a shower of cold water droplets landed on her. Alice glanced upward. Above her, the morning glories had begun to stretch and yawn, shaking off the cold dew. She rose quietly and slipped her nightdress over her head. None of the flowers had noticed her yet, being too preoccupied with stretching their faces to catch the brightest patches of sunlight. Alice crept from the clearing, unwilling to put up with any accusations of being a weed.

Clutching her boots in one hand, she picked her way through the flowerbed, finding the path within moments. She sat upon a large stone, buckling her boots in place. Somewhere ahead Alice could hear a pair of male voices talking quietly. She rose and crept down the path, making her footfalls as silent as possible.

Alice stopped short when she came around a bend. The trail abruptly opened into a large clearing. Donovan was in his feline form, large as a Great Dane with short, scarlet-and-black-striped fur. He sat on one end of a large mushroom, which was red and covered in white splotches. On the other end stood the loveliest moth Alice had ever seen. His enormous wings were a luminous white, each dotted with a pair of silver eyes. In one of his arms he held the mouthpiece of a hookah, though the lack of rising smoke told Alice it wasn't lit.

"How have our people been fairing in my absence?" The cat's tail twitched where it sat, dangling over the edge of the mushroom.

The Moth tapped the tip of the hookah against his mouth, staring at the pretty glass base forlornly. A feathery, white antenna twitched nervously. "Not well, milord. The queen is scouring the land for dissidents, especially 'that wretched, mocking feline.' She has exterminated Dodo's forces, and the March Hare is scheduled for execution in the morning."

The feline paced on top of the mushroom, the worry apparent in his voice. "What of the Hatter? How is he taking the news of Hare's capture?"

"We tried to calm him, milord, but you know how fruitless that is. The Hatter is..." The Moth took a deep breath, trying to get his voice under control. "He heard of the Hare's sentence and lost his head."

"Literally, I would imagine." The seething rage in the feline's voice was obvious. He leaped from the mushroom, pacing over a wider distance on the ground nearby. He stopped suddenly, sitting on the ground. "We must act now, my friend."

The Moth fanned his wings nervously. "But there are so few of us, milord!"

"Yes, and there will be fewer still if we hesitate. Do not fret. There is, after all, a madness to my method."

Alice stepped into the clearing, "Don't you mean 'a method to your madness'?"

The cat looked at her, golden eyes twinkling with mischief. He chuckled softly, fading from view, and appeared in front of her in his human form. He took her hand in his own and raised it to his lips, placing a delicate kiss on her knuckles. "Of course not, my dear. If my plan wasn't mad, it would never work."

The Moth laughed softly. "Have you sorted out who you are yet?"

Alice turned and looked at him for a long moment. "Caterpillar? Why isn't your hookah lit? You seemed to enjoy it so when we last met."

"I tried to light it and nearly scorched my antenna. Apparently, 'a moth to flame' is more than just a saying." The insect shook his head sorrowfully. "Can you imagine the disappointment of it? I spent weeks in my cocoon, fully expecting to emerge as a butterfly, and instead I wind up a common house moth!"

"Well, I think you make a lovely moth." Alice scrambled up onto the mushroom, kneeling by the hookah. She struck a match, blocking the moth's view with her body, and touched it to the brick of charcoal. When it glowed red, she blew out the match. "There."

Alice sat at the edge of the mushroom and slid off as the Moth mumbled a hurried "Thank you!"

She slid off the fungus, Donovan's hands catching her around the waist and gently sliding her to the ground. She smiled at him and blushed, still unaccustomed to the touch of a man, chaste or otherwise.

Donovan took her hands in his own. "Alice, I don't know how much of that you heard, but I cannot allow anyone else suffer because of her tyranny. I need your help."

"The Hatter is truly dead?" Alice's voice broke on the last word. She had always felt a fondness for the madman who had tea with her in her childhood dreams.

Donovan nodded, his eyes reflecting her own sadness. "We need to stop her from harming anyone else."

"Why me?"

Donovan gave her a weary smile, letting her glimpse the toll this was taking on him. "You are the one that escaped her. She has dreamed of recapturing you for thirteen years."

Her eyes met his, and when she spoke, her voice filled with steely determination. "Of course. What do you need me to do?"

He gave her a grin and then slipped a large, golden watch from his pocket. Donovan glanced at its face and let out a weary sigh. "Come, my dear. Not to sound like that blasted rodent, but we must hurry or we'll be late."

"Late for what, Donovan?"

He pulled her into the circle of his arms, the world around them going gray again. She waved good-bye to the Moth, but he sat oblivious in a swirl of blue smoke.

Donovan flashed her a toothy grin just before they Faded, the predatory look returning to his eyes. "Tea, of course. It wouldn't do to keep the Queen of Hearts waiting."

They appeared in a corridor outside of the palace throne room. Alice started toward the huge oak doors, but Donovan hastily grabbed her by the elbow, pulling her back around the corner.

"The Queen thinks me merely another fawning courtier. She has no idea who I truly am." The feline wrapped her in his arms and whispered softly in her ear. "Remember, Alice. I will not allow her to harm you."

Alice caught her reflection in the mirror next to them and froze. She was dressed in the same outfit she had worn upon her first journey to Wonderland. Her powder-blue dress brought focus to her wide, cornflower eyes. Despite the fact she was a grown woman, the outfit lent her a hint of the childish innocence she had possessed on her first journey through the rabbit hole.

She stepped away from Donovan and brushed an imaginary wrinkle from her neatly pressed apron. She bit her lower lip and took a deep breath. Alice took the arm he offered with a nod, allowing him to escort her into the throne room.

Most of the seats in the room were conspicuously empty. The courtiers present all had schooled their faces into carefully neutral masks. Briar was the closest to the dais, and was trying unsuccessfully to hide his nervousness. The look on the poor Rabbit's face bordered on terror, making Alice thankful his back was to the Queen.

The Queen of Hearts sat upon her throne, surveying the room. Alice realized that she must have been beautiful once. She was no longer a young woman; nor was she old. Her jet hair was streaked with silver, and her storm-cloud eyes were filled with the promise of cruelty.

Gone was the throne of the King. Instead, a man sat upon a cushion on the floor by her feet. It took her a moment, but Alice eventually recognized the Knave of Hearts.

Alice leaned over, whispering softly to Donovan, "What happened? Where is the King?"

His ears pressed to her ear. "There was more than raspberry in those tarts. The Knave was ever the Queen's lover, but the King kept her in line by pardoning those she had condemned. Without him, all of Wonderland fell into peril."

The cat squeezed her hand reassuringly and stepped forward, his gait smooth as he sauntered toward the throne. Alice wondered how it was that the Queen had never guessed his identity. Everything in him screamed that he was feline.

Donovan sank to a knee in front of the throne. The Queen's eyes focused upon him, causing Alice's pulse to quicken. "Majesty, I have found her."

The dark eyes focused upon her, and she froze. The pure malice within them caused a shudder to dance along her spine. As the woman's eyes narrowed, Alice dropped into a hasty curtsy. "Your Majesty."

The Queen rose from her throne, her scarlet-and-black skirts swishing softly as she descended from the dais. Alice could see the carefully embroidered hearts that decorated her dress as she moved closer. Her breasts heaved against the tightness of her bodice. As the Queen drew closer, Alice fought against the urge to turn and flee.

Her lips twisted into a parody of a smile. "Ah yes, Alice. Come, child. It's time for tea."

* * *

Alice sat across from the Queen at a small wicker table that overlooked the old croquet field and garden. Clearly, no one was left to tend them. The rose bushes had become a tangled thicket, obscuring the path with a wall of thorns and snowy petals. The croquet hoops, if they remained, were in a field of waist-high grasses and wildflowers. Nearby, the flock of flamingo mallets wandered the edge of the pond aimlessly.

The Queen cleared her throat, causing Alice to fidget nervously in her seat. Though Donovan had assured her that all would be well, her hostess's intense scrutiny weighed heavily upon her. Alice's fingers toyed nervously with the hem of her apron.

"Pardon me, Majesty. I..." Alice trailed off as servant wheeled in a cart and set a saucer and steaming cup of tea in from of each of them. She glanced up at him and quickly hid her shock. The "servant" was none other than Donovan himself. He slunk silently over to the wall behind the Queen and leaned against it, waiting.

He was certainly dressed the part. He wore the belted tunic of a two of clubs, a lowly palace servant. His mahogany hair was tied back, and he even wore white kid gloves. The only thing that gave him away was the calculating look that danced in his strange eyes. Alice took a sip of bittersweet Earl Grey and tried her best not to look in his direction.

"You certainly caused quite a fuss during your last visit." The Queen's voice tore Alice's gaze from Donovan. The Queen delicately sipped from her steaming cup, her eyes still focused upon Alice. "Leaving during your sentencing was quite rude, child."

"I apologize for my behavior, Your Majesty." Despite the dryness in her throat, Alice plucked a tart from the serving tray. Donovan flashed her an encouraging smile and she nibbled on it halfheartedly. She held out the tray for the Queen, who waved it away.

"No... I never eat tarts. " She drained the rest of her tea and gestured absently for a refill. A cruel smile crossed her lips. "We shall, of course, continue your trial promptly after tea. After all, we mustn't leave these things unfinished."

Alice felt herself grow pale, the tart churning in her stomach. "O-Of course not, Your Majesty."

She glanced up at Donovan, who was filling the Queen's cup. He partially filled hers as well, shaking his head subtlety. Alice's gaze dropped to the contents of her cup. The color was slightly redder than the usual hue of Earl Grey.

Clearly, the Queen had failed to notice the change. She raised the cup to her lips and took a long sip. She lowered the cup, glancing at its contents. "Does the tea taste a bit off to you?"

Alice picked up her own cup and lifted it to her mouth, careful not to touch the amber liquid to her lips. She swallowed dryly as Donovan watched her with horrified eyes and then set her cup back on its saucer. "It tastes fine to me, Majesty."

The Queen watched Alice for a moment, her eyes narrowed suspiciously. She tried to keep her face casual, biting into another tart. Her heart pounded loudly as she fervently prayed that the Queen had been fooled by her ruse. She nearly gave a sigh of relief as the other woman took another sip of her tea.

An unpleasant look crossed the Queen's face as she swallowed her mouthful of tea. Alice fidgeted again as the woman sniffed the contents of her cup. "Almond? I despise almond tea!" She rose from her chair, turning with an angry swirl of her skirts. Donovan still leaned against the wall, an arrogant smile upon his lips. He had discarded the uniform in favor of the forbidden, scarlet jacket Alice had first seen him in.

"*You*?" The Queen shrieked the word at the top of her lungs. The cup slipped from her grasp, porcelain shattering on the tile below. She took a few steps in his direction. "Donovan, what is the meaning of this?"

"Indeed, 'me.' Or, should I say..." His voice trailed off as he Faded, leaving only the golden cat eyes and an ever-widening grin. He Faded back in feline form, starting from the tips of his whiskers and ending with the tip of his tail. "Me."

She swayed slightly, as if she was suddenly having trouble keeping her balance. The Queen's face had become a ghostly pale. She opened her mouth as if to speak, but nothing came out.

The Cat laughed, his tone filled with smug satisfaction. "Strange, I didn't think you capable of silence."

She shook her head, as if trying to clear it of imaginary cobwebs. "Guards! Off with his... Off with his..."

The Queen fell to her knees. Strands of her raven-and-silver hair fell across her eyes, but she made no move to brush them away.

The Cat crossed the room slowly, the tension in his body reminding Alice of Dinah stalking a mouse. Halfway to the Queen, he Faded out again, appearing in front of her in his human form. He leaned down and spoke quietly in her ear, "Cyanide certainly tastes like almond, doesn't it, my Queen?"

Donovan straightened and stepped around her, not even sparing a backward glance as she pitched forward onto the tile. He crossed the room to Alice, taking her hand. Fear had returned to his gaze. "Alice, please tell me that you didn't drink that tea!"

"We killed her..." Alice could not seem to shift her gaze from the prone form of the Queen of Hearts.

"Alice, the tea! Did you drink it?" He moved in front of her, blocking her vision. Donovan grabbed her shoulders when she failed to respond. "Alice!"

"What?" She shook her head, snapping out of the numbing shock long enough to meet his panicked eyes. "No. It didn't even touch my lips."

He sighed in relief, wrapping her in his warm embrace. "I could not have survived poisoning you."

"But we killed her..." Alice's voice was a faint whisper as she rested her head against his chest.

"No, love. We saved our kingdom." He shifted her so his arms were wrapped around her shoulders. Donovan led her from the room, giving the corpse a wide berth. Neither of them looked back.

* * *

Alice moved cautiously down a steep, poorly lit stairway, trying not to lose her balance. The tower that had served as the Queen of Heart's prison was freezing and smelled unappealingly of unwashed bodies and mold. Donovan had tried to leave her in the palace below, but she had insisted upon accompanying him. Despite the Queen's soldiers swearing fealty to the Cat, she did not want him alone with them.

They had been led up by a trio of guards to release the March Hare. The three guards were walking ahead and Donovan was carrying the exhausted Hare down the stairs ahead of her, when Alice stopped in her tracks.

"What is it, love?" The Cat paused, glancing back at her.

"I thought I heard something." Alice climbed the few stairs back to the dim passage that held the March Hare's cell. She cleared her throat and called out, "Is anyone here?"

One of the guards had climbed to the landing. "Ma'am, the Queen held executions two weeks ago. The rabbit was the only—"

Alice held up a hand to silence him. She called out again, this time louder, "Is anyone up here?"

Donovan had handed the unconscious Hare to the other two guards and joined her. After a few moments of deafening silence, he gently touched Alice's shoulder. "Are you certain...?"

He trailed off as a faint voice called from a few cells down, "Help..."

Alice sprinted to the cell, fumbling for the key. Her fingers were shaking as she unbolted the door and pushed it open. A familiar purple top hat lay on the ground in front of her. Though it was mangled and crushed, the neatly printed card was still tucked into the band.

Her heart pounded as she stepped into the room. A figure lay against the wall, slumped in the shadows. Alice couldn't bring herself to cross the small space. She called out softly, trying not to succumb to the hope that threatened to overwhelm her. "Hatter?"

"A-Alice? Is it really you?" The Hatter tried to get to his feet and then slumped back against the wall, panting softly.

She raced across the room, sinking to her knees on the foul hay beside him. This close she could see his matted blond curls and the bruises marring his handsome face. His suit was royal purple, though it was filthy and torn. A wilted flower still sat tucked into his breast pocket. He looked as if he had been taken during one of his tea parties.

"Oh, Hatter!" Alice hugged him gently. Tears blurred her vision.

Donovan knelt on the Hatter's other side, smiling at him. "We thought you dead, dear friend."

"I nearly was. The Queen decided to carry out my sentence only after I had witnessed Hare's execution." His voice faltered on the final word. The Hatter's eyes suddenly widened. "Hare! Is he...?"

Donovan touched his shoulder lightly, "He is unconscious, but he will be fine."

Alice noticed a small window cut into the stone wall. Even from here, she could see the executioner's block in the courtyard below. "She truly was insane."

"My dear Alice, when will you learn?" The Hatter's voice was touched by a trace of his usual jovial insanity. "We're all mad here."

Donovan gave a soft laugh. "Some more than others."

She tore her eyes from the window, and her gaze met the Hatter's. His emerald eyes shone with their mixture of madness and mirth, causing relief to flow through her. His lips twitched in a weak smile. "So have you an answer to my riddle? How is a raven like a writing desk?"

In truth, she hadn't given the nonsensical

question much thought since her first Wonderland tea party so long ago. She and Donovan helped the man to his feet, supporting him between the two of them. They took him down the treacherous stairs carefully, pausing to rest at a landing.

Finally, an idea came to her. "Could it be because both of their notes are flat?"

The Hatter's laugh had a haunted edge to it. "Oh, Alice. All of these years and that is the best answer that you can give me? I shall expect a better one when you next come for tea."

* * *

Alice stood inside her chamber, smoothing her skirt and looking at her reflection in the mirror. The bodice of her dress was a layer of transparent black lace, leaving the red chemise she wore beneath peeking through. Her skirt was full and made of black silk. The material had been a gift from the Moth, spun from the remnants of his own cocoon.

Donovan appeared behind her, wrapping his arms around her waist. He kissed her on the cheek and then rubbed his head against hers in a very feline way. "You look beautiful, love. Are you ready?"

At her nod, the world around them dissolved into the nothingness that existed between the two worlds. Glancing up into the branches of the ancient tree, she noticed it was in full bloom. The sweet scent of warming blossoms filled the morning air as she carefully sat down in the grass to wait.

"Alice!" She glanced up to see Susan running

into the clearing, concern lining her face. "Where on earth have you been? I've been beside myself!"

Alice smiled up at her sister, stroking the odd-looking scarlet-and-gray cat that had appeared in her lap. She gently set him on the ground with a whispered apology and rose to her feet. "I came to say good-bye, Susan."

"What are you playing at, Alice? We only have an hour to get you ready for the wedding." Susan took a step toward her sister and then stopped in her tracks as a cascade of pink petals danced through the air around her.

Susan looked up to see the odd cat playfully shaking the flowers from a branch above her. Suddenly, the cat was gone, a handsome man with disconcerting golden eyes appearing in its place. He gave her a rakish grin and then vanished as well. She glanced back at her sister, opening her mouth to speak. The man was standing behind Alice, his arms wrapped around her waist.

Alice pulled away from him and threw her arms around her elder sister. "Wonderland is real, Susan. I'm going home."

Alice stepped back, and the strange man scooped her into his arms. She laughed, throwing her arms around his neck.

Susan glared at them disapprovingly. "Who is he?"

The man inclined his head in her direction, her sister still securely in his arms. "The Cheshire cat, at your service."

As Susan opened her mouth to speak, their forms began to fade. Within a few seconds, all that was left was an enormous grin and a pair of golden feline eyes. Then those winked out as well, leaving Susan standing alone beneath the ancient apple tree.

A Wasp, a Wig and a Wanton Woman
Gary Westfahl

This story is based on "A Wasp in a Wig," the chapter of Through the Looking Glass *that Lewis Carroll removed before publication at the insistence of illustrator Sir John Tenniel.*

As the adult Alice was again walking through the Wonderland she had visited as a child, she came upon a brook, and she remembered that she had leaped over this very brook many years ago, when she had been on her way to becoming a queen. But she also seemed to vaguely recall that just before she leaped, she had met someone... or something. Had it really happened? Had the memory of the event somehow been removed from her brain?

"Excuse me? Are you a female wasp?"

She turned her head to where the voice had come from, and she saw something that looked very much like a very old man... except that his face was more like a wasp's. In fact, Alice shrewdly deduced, he *must* be a wasp, because he had six appendages, four of them serving as arms and two as legs. Alice thought he looked very familiar, sitting on the ground and leaning against a tree; he also was wearing a most conspicuous and incongruous yellow wig on his head. Finally, Alice remembered: she *had* met a wasp very much like this one—perhaps, the same one—in this very place long ago. But for some reason she had never told anyone else about the brief encounter, perhaps because some people might be appalled by the very idea of a wasp wearing a wig. And that might explain why she did not remember it as well as her other adventures.

"I repeat: are you a female wasp?"

At first Alice was a bit indignant to think that anyone, or anything, would mistake an attractive woman like her for a wasp, and her initial impulse was to reply indignantly, "Do I *look* like a female wasp?" But pondering the elderly wasp, she realized that, at least in this part of Wonderland, it seemed that wasps were just as big as people, so she was about the right size to be a wasp, and she also noticed that the wasp was wearing glasses (which were very large indeed, because, as you know, wasps have very large, bulging eyes), so he probably could not see very well at all. And this aroused Alice's sympathy—imagine being unable to tell the difference between a woman and a wasp!

Alice then resolved that she would treat this old wasp the same way she would treat any old man—with great politeness—and she wasn't sure if it was really polite to simply say no in response to his question. So, she decided to avoid an immediate answer and instead asked, "Might I inquire as to *why* you are interested in finding a female wasp?"

"Might you inquire, might you inquire... I would think that it would be obvious! Worrity, worrity!" He raised his four arms as if angered by her response, then abruptly pulled them back near his body. "My old bones, my old bones!" he exclaimed, and Alice recalled that the wasp she had met before (if this was indeed the same wasp) had suffered from rheumatism.

"After all," he continued, "you can see that I'm not as young as I used to be, and a wasp would like to sow his wild oats, you know, and sire a child or two before he passes on. The trouble is, worrity, worrity, female wasps are not as easy to find as they used to be, and I can't really fly very well any more. I'm resting here because I couldn't keep up with the latest scouting party that went out looking for females. So, when I saw you approaching, I was rather hoping that, by some stroke of luck, you would be a female wasp who had come looking for me."

While he was speaking, Alice's eyes wandered down the length of his body, and she was surprised to observe that his dark penis was long and erect, testifying to his great desire for female company. (Of course, Alice thought, it wasn't at all immodest of him to not be wearing pants, because she knew that wasps never wear pants. But Alice had also never heard of a wasp wearing a wig, and she wondered why he had thought to wear a wig but not to wear pants.) His penis did look longer and narrower than a human penis, but that was only to be expected, because he was, after all, a wasp. And in its own way, Alice concluded, it seemed rather attractive.

"Anyway, since you seem unable or unwilling to

answer my simple question, I will say this: if you are indeed a female wasp, I hope you will be willing to enjoy a few moments of intimacy with me. If you are not a female wasp, worrity, worrity, you might, before you go, at least help me read the report from the last scouting party that left in search of females. Even with these glasses, I'm afraid my eyes can no longer read the fine print, and the report might offer a clue, worrity, worrity, as to where I might go next, once I am rested enough to resume my travels."

He gestured toward a newspaper lying at his feet—the *Wasp Street Journal*—and Alice picked it up and began to read out loud. "News. The Exploring Party found what they thought was a crowd of females, lying on a grassy field. They looked a little odd, but their aroma was absolutely scrumptious, and most members of the Party immediately began to pleasure themselves. But the author of this report held himself back, examined the females more carefully and soon realized that they were really—*orchids*! Cunning, treacherous orchids, deluding poor wasps into spilling their seed to no avail!"

Much to her surprise, Alice knew exactly what the report was talking about; for while at university she had taken as her required science class The Natural History of Insects, and the only lecture she now recalled was the only interesting one, about the sex life of insects. The professor had told exactly this story of how some orchids had evolved a way to entice male wasps to mate with them. In this respect at least, it seemed, the flowers of Wonderland were exactly like the flowers of England.

But she saw that the wasp was now gesturing with apparent indignation, and he quickly exclaimed, "Ah, so that's it! You must be an *orchid*—come to deceive one of the few wasps that has not yet fallen prey to your vile perfidy!"

Alice was bemused: while she had initially considered it insulting to be mistaken for a wasp, it was at least a compliment of sorts to be mistaken for an orchid, because Alice had always thought orchids were the loveliest of flowers. But she was becoming rather fond of this crotchety old wasp, and Alice knew that in order for this conversation to continue, she would have to find some way to convince him that she was not an orchid.

She considered some possible strategies. Her first thought was to say, "Oh, come on, dear sir. Do I *look* like an orchid?" But she recalled that this elderly wasp couldn't see very well at all, so that approach wouldn't work.

Then, she pondered saying, "Do I *smell* like an orchid?" But that might be ineffective as well, because Alice had put on some perfume before beginning her journey through Wonderland, and she recalled that it *was* sort of a flowery scent, so it may well be that Alice, in fact, did smell like an orchid.

Another logical objection would have been, "Really, do I *sound* like an orchid? I mean, orchids can't talk!" But Alice knew that in this strange realm, there did, in fact, exist flowers that talked, and Alice had already conversed with some of them. (Though, she mentally added, she was speaking to this wasp *much* more nicely than those flowers had spoken to her!)

86

Finally, she decided that she could appeal to her evident mobility as evidence. "Please, my dear sir, haven't you noticed that I was walking around, and while they might move in the breeze a bit, surely an orchid couldn't do *that*?" (she hoped—though it suddenly occurred to her that if there were flowers in Wonderland that talked, it was also possible that there were flowers that walked.) "Look, I'll walk in a circle around you to prove that I'm not an orchid."

So Alice proceeded to slowly walk in a circle around the wasp, who shifted his cane and tried to turn around in order to keep looking at her. But his clumsy legs couldn't keep up the pace, and he ended up tripping himself and collapsing to the ground.

Alice immediately rushed to the old wasp and helped him get back on his two feet (although she was initially a bit confused as to which two of his six feet she should be helping him get back on). As she held the old man's shoulders, Alice reached a decision. She *did* like this old wasp, and it saddened her to realize that, at his advanced age, he was very unlikely to ever come upon the female wasp that he so dearly craved. So, she resolved to play that role for him and allow him to finally have the pleasure he had long waited for. Why not? It might be fun—it would certainly be *different*—to have sex with an insect, and she couldn't possibly get pregnant from sleeping with a wasp!

She chose her next words carefully. "Look, I know you thought I might be an orchid because I've been so terribly coy about what I really am, but as my mother once cautioned me, a young woman does have to be careful about what information she shares with strangers. But now I've come to know you, I feel I can safely tell you that, yes, I *am* a female wasp, and that I would be most delighted to welcome your advances."

"You are?" he said brightly. Then a suspicious look came over his face. "But you sound rather like a young woman. If you are a wasp, worrity, worrity, you should have been flying around, not shuffling along the ground like an old man. That," he concluded, "is more what a deceitful orchid would be doing, don't you think?"

Alice then remembered another bit of advice from her mother, given when she had become an adult: that you can always distract a man with flattery. "Why, I stopped flying around the instant I saw that there was a very handsome wasp that I could talk to on the ground.

"Anyway, I know the best way to allay your suspicions. I will take off my dress, and you will be able to *see* that I am not an orchid." Alice figured she could get away with this because the old wasp couldn't see well enough to tell the difference, and hopefully while anticipating an amorous encounter he wouldn't think to ask any awkward questions about why someone claiming to be a female wasp was wearing a dress when a male wasp like him wasn't wearing any pants. It did not take her long to remove her dress, her shoes, and all of her undergarments—for she had been getting a lot of practice in doing that during her sojourn in Wonderland.

When she was completely naked, the wasp stared at her and exclaimed, "Ah, yes, watching you move about, and now looking at you, I can indeed tell that you are not an orchid, so worrity, worrity, you must be a wasp. So, with your kind permission, let us proceed to the business at hand." Of course, Alice was enough of a logician to realize that simply proving that you were not an orchid did not prove that you were a wasp, but fortunately the wasp had evidently not been trained in formal logic.

Now, the moment had come. Alice lay down on the ground, which luckily was comfortable enough since there were many leaves to form a cushion of sorts, and the elderly wasp gently positioned his body above her and began caressing her body. Quickly, Alice appreciated the advantage of his having four arms: while his two lower arms were rubbing against her back and her buttocks, the two upper arms were cradling her breasts. It was all, she thought, rather like a threesome. (And if you are wondering why that precise analogy occurred to Alice, suffice it to say that there are experiences in Alice's past that she prefers not to discuss, so I will not discuss them either.) Alice actually felt a bit inadequate because she only had two arms, one to squeeze his behind and the other to gently stroke his penis.

Soon, Alice thought, it was time to proceed to the stage of oral sex—he was, after all, an old wasp, and she wasn't sure how long his erection would last—but as she moved her head down to his penis she felt a twinge of hesitation. It was, after all, an insect's penis, and she had always thought of insects as being rather nasty, dirty creatures. Then, Alice recalled a book her older sister had read to her about a tribe of savages in some faraway jungle that considered insects to be the tastiest of treats, and she proceeded to boldly place her mouth around his penis and start to suck. Alice thought to herself, *Well, I won't be the first person to eat an insect!* She was so delighted and proud of this amazingly witty thought that she almost burst out laughing, but she luckily suppressed the impulse because, as you know, a female should never laugh while she is having sex with a male, since that laughter might be misinterpreted.

After her tongue had caressed his penis for a while, she felt that he was about to come, so she quickly withdrew, lay back down on the ground, grabbed the wasp's throbbing penis, and slowly guided it into her body. She then was pleasantly surprised by his performance, as the wasp pumped back and forth with great enthusiasm for what seemed like the longest time, and Alice soon had not one but two orgasms, which hadn't happened with any of her human lovers for quite some time. For a moment, she wondered: *perhaps, all of these years, I have been wasting my time with the wrong species!*

Only two things about this encounter were rather incongruous. First, Alice was used to hearing the subdued grunting of men as they approached the moment of ejaculation; but as he went about his business, the wasp kept muttering, "Worrity, worrity!" which didn't seem like the proper thing to be saying at all, but perhaps it was the way of all wasps. And at one point during his lovemaking, she suddenly felt a huge mass of hair fall upon her face. Due to the vigor of his movements, the old wasp's wig had fallen off! She threw it aside, and it seemed that the wasp, in the throes of passion, had not even noticed its absence.

Finally, she felt the insect's sperm spilling into her body, and the wasp withdrew from her and lay down beside her. He emitted a long, satisfied sigh, and then—as if it were the most natural thing in the world—he began to recite a poem.

> *There once was a young wasp with pluck,*
> *With women he never had luck.*
> *'Til a gal came along*
> *Who sucked on his schlong*
> *And gave him a wonderful fuck!*

Alice took this in stride because, as she knew from many experiences, the people of Wonderland often expressed themselves in verse. True, she had never heard anyone recite a *limerick* before, but somehow the form seemed eminently suitable for this particular occasion.

Having finished his poem, the wasp then lay back and grew very silent indeed, so much so that Alice grew concerned. Upon standing up to examine her prone companion, she found that his body was cold and stiff. The wasp was dead!

At first Alice felt sad and puzzled, and then she remembered something else the professor had said in his lecture about the sexual habits of insects: that many male insects, after they have sex with females for their first and only time, will immediately die, which had struck Alice at the time as a terribly cruel fate. Now she knew the professor had been correct, based on her own personal experience! (And later, after some further amorous adventures that proved to be less than thrilling,

Alice would rather cruelly wish that some human males, after an unsatisfactory performance, would also die immediately so that no other women would ever have to suffer the displeasure of their company!)

No wonder the old wasp had been so good in bed. After all, if you know that you will only get to do something once in your entire life, you are going to devote every ounce of your energy to making it the very best experience possible. And Alice was glad she had decided to submit to his advances. Perhaps he had died a bit sooner than he otherwise would have, but at least he had died having finally felt the intense sexual pleasure he had craved for so many years.

Now, there was nothing more for Alice to do but put her dress back on and dig a shallow grave for her erstwhile lover. Not knowing what to do with his yellow wig, she stuffed it into her pocket and proceeded to the task. After covering his body with dirt and placing a simple cross on top, she then wondered what sort of epitaph she should write on it.

What happened next would have struck an observer as a very strange thing for a woman who had just finished digging a grave to be doing, but Alice suddenly found it impossible to suppress the urge to giggle. She had remembered a passage from the Bible that she had been made to memorize in school: "O death, where is thy sting? O grave, where is thy victory?" Now that the wasp had fallen into the hands of Death, she thought (while admiring herself for her great cleverness in so thinking), *Death finally had its sting!* And she understood exactly what she should provide as the wasp's epitaph—a clever poem, since they were so common in Wonderland. And this is what she wrote:

> *A wasp in a wig*
> *Such pleasures did bring*
> *Now his grave I dig*
> *And Death has found its sting!*

Perhaps it wasn't really somber enough for the occasion, but it did seem that folks in Wonderland sometimes displayed a rather morbid sense of humor—she recalled that odd poem, "The Walrus and the Carpenter," that concluded with the two gentlemen eating the oysters they had just conversed with—so she decided that whoever might happen to read her epitaph probably would not be overly upset.

Sometime later, having resumed her journey through Wonderland, Alice was extremely distressed to wake up one morning feeling strange and nauseous. Could she possibly be pregnant? She remembered the reasoning that had led her to take no precautions when she had surrendered herself to the wasp, and she had been absolutely correct to believe that, according to all the laws of science that governed the world she lived in, it was completely impossible for a wasp to impregnate a human female. Then again, she had also learned from many experiences that Wonderland was not exactly like the world she lived in. After all, she had carried on conversations with caterpillars, flowers and mice; she had watched herself grow to the size of a giant and shrink to the size of a mouse; she had seen a human baby transformed into a squealing pig.

Obviously, the laws of science really didn't apply in Wonderland, which meant that here, it might be perfectly possible for a woman to give birth to a wasp!

This prompted in Alice's mind a number of vexing questions: does one breast-feed, or bottle-feed, a baby wasp? What schools does a mother send a wasp to, and what does she pack in its lunch? At what age should one allow a wasp to go out on its first date? And what would her mother think about all this? She had recently been dropping some hints that she was looking forward to Alice settling down and giving her some grandchildren to look after, but Alice was sure an adorable little insect was not exactly what her mother had in mind.

Fortunately, Alice did not have to worry about these things for very long, because she found her stomach swelling to an enormous size in just a few more days—which seemed logical enough, since she knew from her class that insects lived much shorter lives than people, which meant that an embryonic insect would naturally take much less than nine months to mature—and one evening, while she was resting on the ground, and while she was fortunately not wearing panties (which, scandalously, was often her habit), she felt something emerging from her vagina, and she looked down to see a little wasp, who looked very much like his father, sitting on the ground in front of her. Feeling that something did not look quite right, she reached into her pocket, pulled out that yellow wig, and planted it firmly on the young wasp's head; he deserved, she thought, to possess some memento from his late father. Calmly accepting the gift, and now looking like a properly attired Wonderland wasp, the baby stood up and flew off into the sky, never to be seen again.

Though she should have been happy to be relieved of what might have been an onerous responsibility, Alice found herself feeling a bit peeved. "Why, he didn't even stay around long enough for me to give him a name!" But she quickly realized it was a very foolish thought, because she had absolutely no idea what sort of name a mother should give to a baby wasp, and she couldn't name him after his father because she had never learned the old wasp's name. Or did wasps even have names? Clearly, Alice did not know enough to properly raise a wasp, so she was left to hope that the poor creature, like other insects, would be sufficiently guided by instinct as to grow up to be a responsible and successful wasp, however a responsible and successful wasp might be defined.

After that time, whenever Alice was asked if she would ever like to have children, she always replied, "Yes, it would be nice to have *human* children," and she always felt a bit sad that she was much too embarrassed to ever explain why that really was a very clever remark.

Wonders Wild and New
Verity Penvenen

The dream-child moving through a land
Of wonders wild and new
—Lewis Carroll, *Alice in Wonderland*

Natasha had barely crossed the street from the office before the torrential rain had plastered her hair to her head. Large, cold drops ran over her scalp, then down her spine, making her shiver. She cursed as a double-decker bus rumbled past and sprayed water over her and three other pedestrians. Natasha forced her way along the crowded pavement, her purple suede shoes audibly squelching as she made her way into the train station. Another colorful curse crossed her lips as she saw that her train was delayed by half an hour. Shivering as her blouse clung wetly to her skin, all Natasha wanted to do was get home and slip into a hot bath.

A fat man with a red, bulbous nose leered at her as he stalked past, then said, "Forgot to watch the weather forecast this morning, did we?" He grinned, and Natasha managed to dredge up a very-funny-now-piss-off smile for him. She *had* watched the forecast—

she had watched for a full five minutes as the forecaster stated how it was going to be a beautiful day with only a few clouds but definitely no rain and there would be no need to take any kind of jacket with you on this sultry July day.

Desperate for something to distract her from this wretched state, Natasha made her way over to her usual magazine kiosk. She found a sign stuck to the door with peeling Sellotape: "Opening soon under new management."

As the third curse of her day was on Natasha's lips, her eyes fell upon the next kiosk along, where piles of tattered books lined shelves stretching from floor to ceiling. Having never noticed it before, Natasha approached and peered into the gloom. She nearly jumped when she saw a pair of glowing, green eyes staring back at her. The eyes moved toward her, and a smiling face was revealed by the lamp on the cashier's desk.

"Feel free to come in and browse," said the man. His eyes seemed less aglow in the full light, yet they were still striking beneath his dark brows. His hair had natural waves, falling with stylish dishevelment over his forehead. His chin had a strong line to it, his nose was straight and his cheekbones softly defined. Yet as Natasha turned to browse, the feature hovering at the forefront of her mind was his smile. As her eyes scanned worn spines, his charming smile seemed to hang in the air before her like an afterimage.

Shaking herself, Natasha focused properly, and one title suddenly struck her among all the others: *Alice in Wonderland*. The name instantly transported

Natasha back to a rainy Saturday afternoon within the first seven years of her life. Grounded for some trivial disobedience, Natasha had wrapped herself in a blanket and sat in the window of their Victorian terrace with the fire in her bedroom blazing. That day, she had first seen the White Rabbit and traveled with Alice into Wonderland.

"Perfect for a rainy evening," Natasha said to herself as she pulled out the battered book. A sullen little girl, a child of Tenniel, cradled a pig in her arms as she stared at Natasha from the cover.

"An excellent choice," said the man behind the counter as Natasha went to pay. "Just the thing for a rainy day."

"True," replied Natasha hesitantly, his echo of her sentiment unnerving her. It was possible he had overheard her murmured words, but doubtful. The look he gave her was piercing, as if he was looking not just into her eyes but beyond them. A shiver went down her spine that had nothing to do with the cold.

"Enjoy your journey," he said as she turned to go.

"My train won't be here for another twenty minutes," she replied.

"Not that journey," he said. His smile broadened into a wide grin, his eyes seeming to sparkle with gaiety and mischief. She stopped herself from shivering again, but only just.

The stench of damp and sweaty bodies on the platform outside soon forced all other thoughts from Natasha's mind. Her train finally arrived, and she managed to find a seat. With a scrawny woman smelling strongly of lavender sitting on one side and a bulky man noisily clearing his throat every few minutes on the other side, Natasha opened her new book and was soon lost in a world of pocket-watches, tarts and curious caterpillars.

The sky was still dark with rainclouds as Natasha unlocked her front door. She felt her luck might be changing when the heavens opened again as she was closing the curtains in her sitting room, safely inside.

After a hot shower and a hasty meal, Natasha curled up in her nightdress on the sofa with a glass of wine and her new book. There was not the sound or shimmer of crackling firelight as there had been when she was younger; the only noise was the antique clock on the mantelpiece, measuring the seconds. As the level of wine in her glass steadily fell, so did Natasha's eyelids. When she reached the Mock Turtle's song, it was like a lullaby and the book fell from her unresisting hand.

When Natasha's eyelids snapped open, she knew something had woken her, but her brain was too sluggish to figure out what. Peering at the clock on the mantelpiece, Natasha saw that it was five minutes past midnight.

Still bemused by what had roused her, Natasha's eyes slid upward to stare at the Waterhouse print above the clock. It seemed somehow both the same and yet unaccountably wrong to her. It took her a good few minutes to work it out: Echo was looking over her left shoulder at Narcissus when previously her chin had rested on her right.

Glancing down at the book lying on the floor, Natasha saw in astonishment that the spine read: *dnalrednoW ni ecilA.*

"What on earth?" she exclaimed, surprised enough to say it aloud. Looking up at the clock again, she saw that the second hand had crept closer to the twelve when reason dictated it should be near the two by now.

"Everything is backward," Natasha murmured in surprise. Carefully she rose and looked out of the window. It was undeniably still raining outside, yet rather than falling downward, the water raced up toward the sky, and Natasha watched in bewilderment as the ground rapidly dried. Before her very eyes, a shaft of golden light burst from the ground below to pierce the clouds above.

This must be a dream, Natasha thought, and such rationalization made the strangeness suddenly easier to accept.

Then Natasha noticed a further difference. The dirty London road and the tower block opposite, which she had stared at so often from her window, had been replaced by the most beautiful garden. Natasha was mesmerized by the sight, holding her breath without even realizing. It was as if a rainbow had fallen to earth and sprouted in the very soil it touched.

"Beautiful," Natasha murmured, filled with a sudden desire to be outside among its magnificence.

Without pausing to put on a raincoat over her nightdress or boots on her feet, Natasha raced down the stairs. She threw open the front door and gasped in shock. The garden she had seen from her window was nowhere in sight. Instead, a forest filled her vision.

Stepping through the door, Natasha felt soft moss beneath her feet. She had hoped the garden might be just beyond sight, but a few tentative steps forward revealed that the forest stretched on to infinity in all directions.

"Where is it?" Natasha said, disappointment etched in her voice.

"Where is what?" asked a voice behind her. Natasha spun round. The shock that she would normally have felt at finding that her home had vanished to be replaced by a gigantic oak was nothing compared to the astonishment of seeing a completely naked man leaning against that same tree. And not just any man, but the man who had sold her the book.

"Where is what?" he repeated. His eyes watched her with interest, a lazy smile playing over his lips.

"T-the garden," Natasha said, embarrassed by his nakedness. She kept her eyes fixed resolutely on his face, but she had already glimpsed the full length of him beneath his smooth, toned torso. Her gaze itched to fall lower.

"Oh, that's the end of your journey," the man said, as if it was patently obvious. Natasha's head swam with confusion. Reaching out, she placed a hand on a nearby tree trunk. She had half expected it to vanish as well, but the smooth bark held firm beneath her touch.

"Journey?" she asked.

He pushed himself away from the oak tree and walked toward her. He moved with a predatory elegance, reminding Natasha of a cat stalking through long grass.

"Yes," he replied simply. "You are about to go on a journey, and that was the end."

"That makes no sense," Natasha replied. "How can you start a journey by being at the end?"

"But how can you get to where you're going if you don't know where it is or what it looks like?" the man questioned. He raised one elegant eyebrow.

It felt to Natasha as if her rational mind had hung up a notice: "Back in five minutes," and her brain had moved into autopilot. If she tried to force open that locked door, her mind would rail against such intrusion. It seemed the most sensible option was to merely go with the flow of this most peculiar dream.

"I guess that makes sense," Natasha said slowly.

"Of course it does," the man said. "You just never thought of it that way before. You'll find a lot of things here make sense, just not in a way you're used to."

"Where is here?" Natasha asked. The dizziness that had accompanied her confusion was beginning to ebb, but a new sensation washed over her as he stopped in front of her. Placing one arm above his head on the same tree as Natasha, he was so close that she could almost feel the heat radiating off him.

Or more likely, she thought, *I'm just blushing from having a naked man standing so close. Not that me in my nightdress is any more decent, of course.*

The man was slightly taller than she was, so that when she looked straight ahead, her gaze lingered on his lips. They were full, curved, and parted ever so slightly. His breath smelled of warm milk and sweet honey. From a distance, she had seen that his body was muscled and lithe. Up close, she could have seen every dark hair on his smooth chest if she had allowed herself to glance down.

"This has to be a dream," Natasha said resolutely. Pushing herself away from the tree, she turned her back on the man before temptation got the better of her.

"If you want it to be," said the man, following close behind.

"What do you mean?" Natasha demanded, determined to hold on to logic, if nothing else. "Either this is a dream or it isn't. Which is it?"

"Neither or both. Are things really so clear-cut in your world?" he asked.

"Yes," Natasha answered defiantly. "Well, mostly," she amended.

The man stood in front of her. "I bet they're not," he said. His eyes held a challenge. Natasha seized the opportunity to channel the arousal his proximity was fueling within her into another emotion. She rose to his challenge.

"Yes, they are," she said. "In my world, buildings stay where they are, forests know their limits, and men wander around with clothes on."

"Cat," the man corrected before he turned and walked away. Natasha frowned, then hurried to catch up to him.

"Cat?" she asked.

The man stopped. "Yes?" he said, looking at her.

"Where is there a cat?" Natasha asked, thoroughly confused.

The man looked at her as if she was stupid. "Right in front of you," he said. For a moment, Natasha wondered if maybe the world had shifted again, but then she realized what he was implying.

"You're trying to tell me you're a cat?" she asked incredulously. The man beamed at her, a true Cheshire grin. Natasha paused, as someone might pause and look down before they throw themselves down a waterfall. "So, are you trying to tell me that you're the Cheshire cat, and this is Wonderland?"

"Got it in several!" said Cat happily. He walked past her, continuing down the slope. Natasha found herself hurrying after him again. She caught him standing by the edge of a deep but clear river.

"Does that make me Alice, then?" she asked as he moved toward a boat. He looked back at her as he untied the mooring rope.

"Definitely not," he said. "She was much shorter than you." He got in the boat and sat down. He looked at her expectantly. "Are you coming or not?"

Natasha glanced behind her. Reason dictated that she ought to return the way she had come and try to find her house. Or even that beautiful garden. Even Cat had said that was end of her journey, the way home. His voice called out from the boat, as if he were reading her thoughts. "Reason says that you can't end your journey until you have begun it, Nat."

She signed, resigned. Yet, as the cool shallows of the river lapped at her ankles, the spark of adventure and excitement ignited in her breast.

"Don't call me Nat," she said reproachfully as she stepped into the boat. It drifted away from the bank of its own volition.

"Why not?" he asked. "Nat and Cat. Or, since you're about as irritating as a bug buzzing in my ear, maybe it should be Gnat and Cat." Natasha looked at him. His words might be harsh, but his tone was good-natured.

Refusing to be won over by his indolent smile, and determined not to let her eyes wander to what lay between his splayed legs, Natasha diverted her attention to the water that flowed around the small boat. She gasped as she looked into the depths.

Figures, both male and female, shimmered beneath the surface. As the water rippled, so did their limbs. As the weeds beneath them swayed in the current, so their bodies writhed and wriggled, all of them as naked as her companion. Natasha watched in prudish horror as legs parted thighs, hands caressed breasts, and one male figure pushed three translucent fingers inside the female arching beneath him. Natasha scrambled to the other side of the boat, but the scene beneath the water was of the same tone. One male figure's moans of ecstasy were lost in bubbles as he was impaled by another male behind him. One female was lying in a bed of green weeds, a male figure on either side of her. One of them was nibbling her ear, his fingers squeezing and tweaking her nipple; the other had his lips clamped over her other nipple, his back to Natasha. When the second male moved to mount the female, she opened her eyes wide and stared straight at Natasha. As he thrust into her, the female cried out in pleasure, then grinned and winked at Natasha before the next thrust sent a second spasm of satisfaction through her watery limbs.

"It's all so..." Natasha began, turning back to her companion, but the boat was empty.

"All so what?" called a voice from the bank.

Natasha saw that Cat was standing there, tugging on the rope and guiding the boat toward its mooring.

How on earth did he get over there? she thought in surprise. *It's surely too far for him to jump, and even if he did, the boat would have rocked at least a little. Or maybe he just vanished and reappeared again, like so many things around here.*

Natasha thought about asking, but she knew she would get little sense out of him. He reached out a hand to help her out of the boat and then held on to her once she found her footing. The words telling him to let her go were on the tip of Natasha's tongue, but her throat was constricting with desire and keeping them in. The part of him she had so deliberately been avoiding looking at was pressed against her. She could feel the heat and the length of him against her thigh, and she felt her own sex become slick with desire.

"You should put some clothes on," she said as forcefully as she could.

He grinned. "Maybe you should take some off. Surely that makes just as much sense?" he replied. There was no answer to that—at least, no answer Natasha trusted herself to give—so she merely wrenched her hand out of his and walked off. She waited a few paces away and he took the lead.

"Where are we going?" she asked.

"I'll show you when we get there," he responded. Although his back was toward her, she could hear the smirk in his words. She rolled her eyes in exasperation and found that they came to rest on his arse. She tried to drag her gaze away, but it was hypnotizing watching those pert buns rising and falling with each step. Before she could help herself, her mind's eye had placed those firm cheeks between her open thighs, rising and falling as he thrust in and out of her. She imagined her foot curling around the back of his calf, running up his skin to meet the sweat that was running down.

"It's rude to stare, you know," whispered a voice in her ear. Natasha shook herself out of her fantasy to find that Cat was no longer in front of her. Instead, he was standing so close behind her that his chest brushed against her with each indrawn breath.

How does he do that? she thought, as angry and ashamed as a little girl who has been found with her fingers in the jam.

"I wasn't staring," she said quietly.

"Well, you should be," he retorted. "Look." He pointed ahead of them, where a circle of bushes formed the outer ring of a clearing. A great raucousness was coming from the clearing. Curious despite herself, Natasha crept forward and parted the bushes so she could peek through.

Two figures were caught in a dire wrestling match. Both wore tattered clothes, one of the purest white and one of gold. As the pair struggled round, each trying to throw the other off-balance, Natasha gasped in recognition.

"That's Bernice and Alan!" she said, her voice quiet but squeaky with restrained shock.

"No," said Cat, creeping up to crouch behind her. "That's the Lion and the Unicorn. They've fought all round the town, and still they aren't sated."

"But, it's Bernice and Alan," insisted Natasha,

mesmerized by the scene before her. Bernice, her snooty office manager, was now panting and struggling before Natasha's eyes. The pristine white trouser-suit she often strutted around in was now hanging from her in tatters.

Poised against Bernice, the strain showing on his face, was Alan, the company accountant. His lips, normally parted in a sneer whenever Natasha handed in her end-of-month reports, were now curled in a snarl as he tried to wrestle Bernice to the ground. His hair, normally so neat and oiled, was longer and mussed up so that it plastered around his face and neck like a mane.

"I guess some things are the same here after all," commented Natasha, smiling as she watched them. "Bernice and Alan are always at each other's throats in my world. They positively hate each other."

"Really?" asked Cat, a mocking tone in his voice. Natasha was about to protest when the match before them reached a turning point. Bernice lost her footing and tumbled to the ground with a cry. Alan threw his head back and let out a loud roar before he fell on her, ripping the remaining rags of clothing from her body. Then, as she clasped him in her arms, he mounted her and the pair began rutting right there in the clearing like a pair of true animals. Natasha watched openmouthed as Alan's body rocked backward and forward while Bernice raked her manicured, crimson nails down his back.

"Strange, I always thought it was the unicorn which had the horn," said Cat behind Natasha. She watched as the true definition of a screaming orgasm was acted out in front of her. She felt Cat move behind her, and she turned to see him walking away. With one last disbelieving look into the clearing, she scrambled up and hurried after him.

"What on earth was that?" she demanded, grabbing his arm and spinning him to face her. He looked at her in surprise.

"Didn't you ever guess what lay beneath their fighting?" he asked. "I thought it was clear-cut in your world. Surely their desire for each other was evident?"

"Never," replied Natasha. They began walking along side by side. Natasha considered what she had seen. "They fought so much; I never guessed that it hid something deeper. They seemed to be so good at the fighting."

"Everyone's different," replied Cat in a wise voice. "Some find that the heat of anger is much the same as the heat of passion. What do you find passionate, Nat?"

Natasha avoided his eyes. In truth, it had been so long that she had forgotten. So many other things had taken precedence recently: her job, her night classes, her plain exhaustion. She barely remembered the last time she had indulged in sex, and she definitely couldn't remember the last time she'd lost herself the way Bernice and Alan just had. Cat waited expectantly beside her.

"Lots of things," she said defiantly after a pause.

"Excellent. Then you should enjoy it here," announced Cat. "What about this?" Cat led her through the trees until they came to a grotto. There was a small stream snaking its way through the center, bubbling up through a set of smooth, gray stones. On one of the larger stones near the source sat a large man, his fat jowls quivering with pleasure as a nubile, young woman and a toned man undressed him.

"That's Phil from the bank across the road," Natasha whispered to Cat. "He's the most lecherous old fart I've ever seen. He always stares at your arse or your tits when you're talking to him, or even when you're just walking past."

"Ah, a man who takes every pleasure as and when he can in life," Cat said with an approving nod. Natasha gave him a disapproving frown, but he merely grinned back at her. "Yet there is one thing that our dumpty little man really enjoys..."

Natasha turned sharply to Cat. "Did you say 'dumpy' or 'dumpty'?" she asked.

"Yes, that's exactly what I said," Cat replied. Natasha rolled her eyes in exasperation, then turned her attention back to the rotund form of Phil. She was surprised at her own eagerness to see the scene unfold. As disgusted as she was at this new, voyeuristic side to herself that was emerging, there was no denying it. An undeniable ache had begun in Natasha's belly when she had watched the lion and the unicorn. Now, as she watched the young man and woman undress Phil then themselves, that ache began to send smoldering tendrils lower down her body.

"What's he saying?" Natasha whispered to Cat as a completely naked Phil set the young girl on his knee.

"He's reciting poetry," Cat said. Natasha strained to hear, and although she could not make out many of the words, the rhythm of his fevered whisperings to the girl was undeniably poetic.

Natasha watched as the young man moved to

kneel behind Phil. The girl was giggling as Phil muttered lyrical obscenities in her ear. She leaned down to stroke his manhood. Natasha had to strain forward to see it, so tiny and hidden by the fleshy folds of his belly above. Yet, despite its tiny size, it stood firm and twitched in the young girl's hand.

As the bud between her own legs began to tingle and burn, Natasha felt an overwhelming urge to lower her hand and allow her fingers to play across it. She resisted, part of her brain yelling at just how perverted and un-Natasha-like it would be to succumb to such desires. And yet a much greater part of her mind was whispering just how delightful it would be.

"I didn't know Phil liked men as well as women," she commented distractedly to Cat.

"Phil likes poetry, words both filthy and pure— the person he's whispering them to is almost irrelevant," Cat replied. He turned then to look her straight in the eye. "Do you like words, Natasha?" he asked with a sly smile. "Does it get you deliciously hot when a man whispers in your ear exactly what he is going to do you?"

Natasha blushed and turned away. It had never appealed to her before, but the ecstasy etched on Phil's face was beginning to change her opinion. As she watched, the girl gripped Phil's shaft harder, massaging it with dexterous fingers. Phil's recitation paused for a groan of pleasure, then he redoubled his efforts. The man kneeling behind Phil had one arm draped over his shoulders and was caressing and tweaking Phil's nipples. His other hand was hidden, but the movement of his shoulder suggested to

Natasha that he was pleasuring himself. The young man's eyes were closed as he drank in the words with as much pleasure as Phil took in spouting them.

Snatches of the poetry drifted as far as Natasha's ears—lyrical descriptions of anatomy interspersed with obscene words and exclamations. The pitch of Phil's voice and the passion of his recitation increased to a fever pitch as the woman rubbed his cock faster and harder. Natasha saw Phil begin to arch his back, pointing his prick in the air to enable the young woman to reach all the way to the hilt of him. Yet the movement unbalanced him and he tumbled backward. From the simultaneous cry of surprise from Phil and the one of pleasure from the young man behind him, Natasha knew Phil's buttocks had slipped over the young Adonis's own penis.

Phil tried to struggle up, but the young man wrapped his arms around Phil's chest and began pumping behind him. Even as Phil's protest died on his lips, chased away by a dazed smile of newfound pleasure, the young woman climbed astride him. She rocked backward and forward on Phil's shaft. Penetrated from behind and mounted from the front, Phil was incapacitated by pleasure, and he rode the storm of both of them with shrieks of orgasmic joy.

The three of them moaned and screamed their way to a climax before falling in a heap of twitching, satisfied flesh. Natasha tried to ignore the burning need in her own loins that this scene had evoked as she turned to Cat. She gasped in shock to find him watching the scene intently, his fingers delicately playing along the length of his own fully erect cock.

Natasha had avoided looking straight at his manhood, yet now her eyes were irrepressibly drawn to its smooth length. It was flushed with blood, and a teardrop of moisture balanced on the tip. A sudden desire blazed within her to reach out and touch him, to stroke him. She struggled to chase such thoughts away.

"That really is uncalled for," she said in forced anger, standing up and stalking away. "It's invasion of privacy or something. Can we leave now?" She stood with her arms folded, her shoulders tense with resolve, and waited for him. The nightdress that covered her brushed uncomfortably against her hardened nipples.

"Not to your taste?" inquired Cat, sidling up next to her. His expression held no mockery, only genuine interest.

"What, you mean that orgy or your reaction to it?" she asked haughtily.

"Either. Both. I only want to find out what drives you, Natasha. Don't you want to find out too?"

"I already know, thank you very much," she replied. Suddenly all she wanted to do was find that beautiful garden, walk through it breathing in deeply the scent of the flowers—to be at peace in this strange world before going home. "Shall we move on?" she asked and started walking.

They proceeded in silence for a short way before they came to a crossroads. Natasha looked up at the sign, which pointed three separate ways. She read the destinations aloud.

"New Unexpected. Dangerous Dark. Safe Secure. What strange place names they have here," she murmured. She turned to ask Cat about them, but he had vanished.

"Such an irritating habit," Natasha said under her breath. "Well, the choice seems simple. I don't like surprises, and I'm not going to choose any dark road, so I guess 'Safe Secure' is the way to go."

Natasha walked in the direction the arrow pointed. She kept up a brisk pace until she came to another set of crossroads. Glancing up at the signpost, she found the same three options. Natasha looked around curiously, but nevertheless followed the direction of "Safe Secure." In time, she came to another crossroads.

No, she thought, *it's not another one: it's the same one. This dratted thing is sending me round in circles!*

"What do you expect when you only choose the safe road? You never go anywhere new or interesting." It was Cat's voice, but although she peered carefully into the surrounding forest, there was no sign of him.

"Well, that's very helpful, isn't it?" said Natasha loudly. When there was no response, she sighed. "Then I guess I'd better choose a different road if I want to get home. I still don't fancy anything dangerous, so I guess it's 'New Unexpected' this time."

Natasha followed the path, which wound past a selection of clearings and grottos. Although each was shielded by undergrowth, there was nothing to stop the moans, giggles, and cries of couplings from reaching her ears. Natasha resisted the urge to peek into any of them, keeping her eyes fixed on the path before her. She tried to fill her mind with images of the garden, of how wonderful it would be when she reached it, but the noises still tugged at the edge of her imagination.

Finally, curiosity overcoming her better senses, Natasha snuck forward and peered into the next clearing she came across. Within in it she saw two naked men wrestling each other. One wore a white sash, one a red. Natasha could see that this wasn't like the wrestling match between the lion and the unicorn. There was real fury in the faces of these men, and, when the two of them staggered to one side, Natasha saw why. Sitting on a mound of grass, eagerly watching the tussling men, was Jane, the office receptionist. The men Natasha recognized only as two of the many men who were constantly hanging around her flirtatious colleague.

Jane sat there naked, her eyes sparkling as she watched the action. Her shoulder-length hair, always smooth and silky, reached all the way to her ankles, pooling on the ground next to her. Natasha was unsurprised to hear Cat's voice behind her.

"Does this appeal to you, Natasha? Men fighting over you? Or do you just prefer the one? Is it quality or quantity you look for?"

"Perhaps not those men," Natasha said evasively. She heard a low chuckle behind her. She did not give Cat the satisfaction of turning round to see whether or not he was actually there.

The scene in front of her changed as the man with the white sash threw his opponent to the ground. Jane laughed and clapped at her knight's victory, then opened her arms to him. The white knight rushed to her side, burying his face in the flesh between her breasts. As he planted a dozen fevered kisses on her skin, Jane lay back on the grass and sighed with pleasure.

"This scene is not as much of a surprise as the others," murmured Natasha. "Even in my own world, Jane is a terrible flirt." Yet that truth did nothing to lessen the desire that crept through Natasha as once again she played the voyeur. She watched with bated breath as the white knight's kisses traveled across Jane's breasts.

As her victor suckled at her nipple, Jane beckoned the fallen red knight. He crawled over to her as the white knight took his kisses lower. When her champion buried his face between Jane's legs, she gasped in pleasure. Writhing beneath the white knight's questing tongue, Jane reached out to the red knight beside her. Her hand crawled across his skin, seeking out his shaft, which stood as proud as a lance.

While the white knight's tongue plunged in and out of her, lapping and circling at the skin of her vulva, Jane gripped the red knight's cock in her hand and began stroking hard and fast.

The white knight was oblivious to the attention his fallen opponent was receiving. His whole being was focused on drinking deeply of the juices that flowed from between Jane's legs. He lapped and sucked, Jane moaned and writhed and the red knight's thighs tightened as Jane brought him closer to climax.

Natasha watched the frenzied trio with a rising desire of her own. She fought to control it, but then she felt fingers behind her tracing a line across her buttocks. The fingers slipped beneath her nightdress, stroking around her skin to find her little, hardened mound. Natasha gasped, then gritted her teeth as a single digit drew circles around her clitoris, spreading heat through her loins.

Eventually overcome with desperation to sate the desire within her, Natasha tried to move her hips back against Cat. With a dark chuckle, Cat's finger swiftly withdrew and there was nothing but empty air behind her. As the group in the clearing yelled out their satisfaction, Natasha was left alone and shaking with frustration.

Natasha set herself a brisk pace after that, her face flushed with arousal. She wanted to leave all these clearings and their temptations behind. At one point, she did allow herself to turn to see if Cat was following her, but the path behind was empty. Turning back, she found a door facing her. There was no wall, no fence; just a solitary wooden door in the forest. She was sure it hadn't been there a moment before.

She walked all around it and found nothing unusual. She opened it toward her and saw the same forest through its frame. Closing the door, she walked around to the other side and opened it away from herself to reveal the beautiful garden she had been seeking all this time.

Natasha cried out in joy and stepped through the door. The scents that swirled around her were just as potent as she had imagined. The sound of sweet birdsong and the soothing gurgle of a stream brought serenity to her mind.

She wandered as if in a daze, and it was some moments before Natasha realized that the flowers around her were moving, and not just with the breeze brushing over them. Looking around, Natasha saw each flower had a face and a body. They were entwined, sighing as zephyrs played over their colorful skin.

Natasha stopped before a flowerbed that she was certain was full of daisies, lisianthus and narcissi. Yet she also saw that they were in fact three women: one with a body as golden as the sun, one with amethyst skin and the third a lighter golden color with pure white hair. The violet woman looked up at her and grinned.

"Would you like to join us, Natasha?" she asked. "Are you tired of simply watching?" The other two giggled and held out their hands encouragingly.

"There can be a lot of pleasure in simply watching," Natasha replied, her voice hoarse, her mind uncertain. The golden woman reached up and stroked a finger down Natasha's arm.

"True, but we can show you so much more pleasure than that," she said with a fiendish smile.

With a nervous anticipation, Natasha allowed them to lay her down between them. As she closed her eyes, they stroked her skin, their fingers as soft as flower petals. They undressed her, combed her hair, kissed her cheeks and ran their hands over every part of her. Natasha was adrift in a sea of delicate sensation, and when she thought it could get no more blissful, a shadow fell across her.

Opening her eyes, Natasha looked up to see Cat towering above her. His shaft was as eagerly erect as ever, and this time she let her eyes linger on it. Her tongue ran across her dry lips as he knelt down in front of her.

"What a pretty picture," he murmured.

"But missing something," Natasha said, suddenly bold. The decidedly immoral smile he gave her reached all the way to his eyes.

Cat leaned over Natasha, planting a delicate kiss on her lips. She was overwhelmed with the scent and warmth of him. Her skin prickled as he ran his fingers over her breast and her stomach before he sought out her round mound again.

As his fingertips brushed over it and slid inside her, Natasha gasped and arched her back. She felt his cock pressing into her thigh, and she reached down to grab it firmly. Cat smothered her mouth with kisses as first one finger, then two slipped in and out of her. Natasha met his kisses with a fiery passion, and her hand slid up and down the full length of his shaft.

Removing his fingers from within her, Cat took hold of her hand and moved it away from his cock. He ceased kissing her and looked into her eyes with a wicked grin. Flooded with desire and frustration, Natasha was desperate for him to plunge into her hard and fast. Instead, Cat entered slowly, making her feel every inch of him until he was buried within her. Natasha tried to move her hips, but he held her firm, withdrawing from her equally slowly. Natasha moaned, digging her nails into his back as he continued to move achingly slowly.

"I think I've found what fuels my desire most in this world," Natasha managed to gasp, her voice shaking. Cat paused and looked at her. The strain of holding himself back showed in his face.

"Really? What's that?" he asked. She gave a throaty laugh.

"Why, you, Cat," she said. His grin almost split his face in two. He slid inside her again, in and out, but faster now. Each thrust brought Natasha closer to her climax, her sex burning with the heat of friction and passion as Cat drove furiously into her.

As the wave of orgasm broke over Natasha, colors danced behind her eyelids and her whole body felt aflame with sensation. She cried out, her own peak bringing Cat to his at the same time. They moaned and shuddered as passion rocked them to their very souls before gently receding.

Cat slid off her, then cradled Natasha in his arms until the exhaustion of their passion overcame her and she slept. When she opened her eyes again a short while later, Natasha expected to see ferns of forest green, flowers like rainbows and colorful, smiling faces. The world that met her eyes was much darker than she had expected. She sat up in surprise.

"I'm home," she said, although there was no one to hear her words. She felt both sadness and relief at this. It took great effort to heave herself off the sofa and drag herself into bed, but once there, she was asleep instantly.

The light of the morning eventually awoke Natasha, and her journey into Wonderland seemed nothing but a strange memory. A strong cup of coffee and a hot shower made the weird and wonderful world slip even further away.

Walking through her living room, Natasha picked up the book that had fallen from her hands the night before. She gave it a nostalgic smile. As the pages fluttered open, a small business card fell out. Natasha picked it up and stared at it for some time. Then she dialed the number from the card.

"Hello, Mark's Secondhand Books," rang out a familiar voice on the other end.

"Hello Ca—" began Natasha, then corrected herself before she made a serious error. "Er, sorry. Hello. I see you also have a store on Shirland Road. What are your opening times, please?"

"Is that the lady that bought *Alice in Wonderland* yesterday?" asked the voice. Natasha was taken aback but saw no reason to deny anything.

"Yes. I bought it from the station."

"Ah. Well, in that case, we're open until four, and then there's a small Italian coffee shop round the corner you can take me to."

The cheek! Natasha thought, but she could hear the smile in his voice.

"Fine," she said brusquely, knowing he could undoubtedly hear her own smile. "I'll see you then." As Natasha replaced the receiver, she allowed her smile to grow a little larger until a wide, Cheshire grin covered her face.

If This Be Not Love, It Is Madness
Theresa Sand

When Mary Ann saw the Mad Hatter kissing the White Knight, she knew he was not mad.

They were in the alcove of the Hatter's little home. She had a letter from the White Rabbit stuffed in her apron, and she had walked into the Hatter's house with angel's trumpet in her hair. It was only dawn, but she was already late. Her mind was a whirligig of tasks and chores, which the White Rabbit deemed unimportant in comparison to the delivery of his numerous letters of many shapes and sizes (sometimes ones so small she had to pinch them between thumb and forefinger).

But all those thoughts vanished as soon as she witnessed the Hatter and White Knight in a passionate embrace. She was so shocked she dropped her basket of mushrooms. She was light on her feet, but her voice carried (the White Rabbit was always shushing her), and her gasp caused the White Knight to break away from the kiss.

The Hatter said nothing, lax in his repose against the wall. His eyes remained shut even as the White

Knight stumbled around the room in search of his sword and his armor. He mumbled his apologies and bashed his knee against the table before ducking out of the house, his armor piled up in his arms.

Still the Hatter did not move, or speak. His hat was on the floor, and his black hair was mussed. He was a beautiful man but hid it with ill-fitting clothes and unkempt hair. Mary Ann often found herself daydreaming about what he must have looked like when he was a singer at the Queen of Hearts' court, dressed in gilded finery, his raven hair brushed away from his face, revealing his high cheekbones and generous mouth.

"Mary Ann," he greeted softly, his lips quirked into a smile. "If you like to watch, you should have come earlier."

He turned his head, opened his eyes, and set her in his clear, obsidian stare.

She ignored the rush of heat to her cheeks, grabbed her basket, and strode over to the dusty alcove, the letter in her free hand. She halted in front of him, ignoring the rapid beat of her heart. It was always that way when in close proximity to the Hatter, and she chided herself for it. She was widowed. She had a child. She was not old, but she was hardly a silly girl.

The Hatter stared down at the letter between them, considering before he plucked it from her fingers. His fingertips grazed her hand, and she snatched it back as if he had burned her.

"Is this from the White Rabbit?" he asked. His voice was melodious and low, as if ready at any moment to break into song.

Mary Ann ignored her surprise at such a simple question. The Hatter never asked them. He preferred riddles and rhyming. After Alice, he had sunk into stranger behavior and proclaimed that Time, in even greater revenge of his attempted murder, had moved him forward to midnight. The tea party was abandoned, save for the Dormouse, who dozed against a cobwebbed teapot, singing nursery rhymes in his sleep.

"Of course," she said finally.

The Hatter raised one inky eyebrow. "No course but progress, Miss Mary."

"Ann," she finished.

"Two names for one woman." He sighed and tapped the edge of the letter against his forehead. "You must be a handful." His eyes drifted down her body, and the implication was obvious.

She felt herself flush again. It irritated her, and added to her irritation over the fallen basket of mushrooms, her tardiness and the rush of desire she had felt when she watched the White Knight and Hatter kiss.

"You must be lonely," she blurted out, immediately regretting her statement.

He pursed his lips. "Must I be an emotion?"

"Of course," she stammered.

"There you go again. You are not very contrary, are you, Mary?"

"You need to be careful," she advised hotly, angry at herself. "If the Queen of Hearts were to find out about—"

"About what? The actions of a madman?"

"I know that isn't true."

"Oh?" He yawned. "What is true and what are lies? The only thing you can be sure of is neither can be bread pudding." He grinned again. "My, my, Mary Ann, you have put me in a tizzy. Perhaps I should throw a little party to show my recent assignations are not at all as treacherous as you would imply."

"I would never—"

"*Never* is a horrible word, Mary Ann. So absolute, so unwavering." His smile widened. "Yes, a dinner party is what I shall throw—so high up in the air all of the Land shall see it." He glanced down at her, and his gaze changed. She suddenly noticed his hands were empty.

He cupped her face, his thumbs caressing her jaw. She was shocked into stillness.

"I'm ravenous just thinking about it," he murmured.

She swallowed, unable to speak. He had moved imperceptibly closer to her, their hips aligned, the heat of his body seeping into hers. Being this close she noticed a small scar by the corner of his right eye. She wanted to rest her fingers on it, but instead her hands fisted by her sides. He was playing with her, and she would not be fooled, not even as his beautiful, dark eyes stared down so deeply into her own.

"Haven't you had your fill?" she said, suddenly angry.

"Never," he explained calmly. "I'm a bottomless well."

"A well isn't ravenous."

"Don't be so sure," he said.

He pressed his lips against hers, his thumbs pressing lightly against her jaw, opening her to the sudden invasion of his tongue. She grasped the lapels of his dusty dinner jacket, nearly sinking to her knees as his tongue swept over her teeth. His arm circled around her waist and anchored her against his hard body. His other hand threaded through her hair, scattering angel's trumpet to the floor.

She was lost in a wave of passion, thrown against the cliffs. His tongue touched hers, coaxing her reply, and she answered, tentative, until his hand slid from her hair to her breast. She froze against his mouth, shocked by his blatant touch and by her own uninhibited response.

"Next time," the Hatter whispered against her lips, "you should knock."

* * *

Mary Ann had loved her husband. They had married very young; she was an orphan, and so his family became her own. He gave her a home and a daughter. He surprised her with primroses and kisses. But then he went to war. He died.

Mary Ann did the best, the only thing, possible. She left her daughter with her husband's parents and took a position as the White Rabbit's housemaid. She was subject to his whims and paranoia. Often her hands would go stiff from washing and ironing his hundreds of gloves, but she was content to know her child was safe.

She tried to focus on that fact each day, especially now, stuck in the Hatter's dank kitchen. It was the day of his promised dinner party, and she was in charge of his servants: a lazy lot who would not care if one of their own drowned in a bucket. In fact, the Dormouse had almost done just that, and Mary Ann had to yank him out. He sputtered a thanks before dragging his sopping-wet body to the dining room, where the Duchess's Frog-Footman had established himself. The Frog-Footman had given Mary Ann a mocking bow, followed by a roll of his large eyes. Mary Ann made a mental note to add extra salt to his dinner.

The Hatter was in fine form, meaning that his madness was in tip-top shape. He had already broken ten dishes after deciding his dinner party should sit on the floor. He had turned the richly embroidered tablecloth into a linen fortress and demanded everyone sit beneath it so that "The Moon's clever eyes will not spy upon our secrets."

Everyone had done as he asked, and Mary Ann, in her scurrying back and forth, detected that the Hatter's guests were pleased that he was back to his old self.

The White Knight was not there, and Mary Ann found that she was happy for it. But when the March Hare arrived (four hours late), the party immediately took a somber turn. When she brought out the third teapot, the tablecloth was back on the table, and every plate (broken or not) had been returned to its spot.

"March Hare has tired of my games, it seems," the Hatter sighed.

Mary Ann walked by him, and his hand shot out, lightning quick, ensnaring her wrist. She halted and ignored the heat that ran up her arm, the amused look on the Hatter's face.

He pulled her close, until she was behind the table and next to his seat.

"Tell me, Mary Ann. Do you think the March Hare is angry at me?"

Mary Ann glanced down the table, where the March Hare blinked at her blearily. In fact, the whole party looked worse for wear; the Duchess's head had fallen in her soup bowl. Only the Frog-Footman was alert, glaring at her from his post by the door.

"I think—" she swallowed at the Frog-Footman's narrowed eyes "—*sir*. That he is too drunk to be much of anything."

"Much of anything? Much of anything!" the Hatter crowed. He dropped her wrist, but before she could make an escape, he twisted his fingers in the bottom of her dress, tethering her to his side.

"Well then." The Hatter put a finger to his lips. "That is much more than he was before." He leaned forward. "Isn't that right, *March Hare*?"

Mary Ann felt as if a weight had dropped in her stomach. Something wasn't right. The Hatter was not crazed: he was angry, and it seemed as if his dinner party was the subject of his rage. What had happened to make him so angry?

Her thoughts raced in every direction as she felt the weight of the Hatter's hand drop from her dress and edge up her skirt. His fingers settled on her leg, his thumb brushing the soft underside of her knee. Mary Ann suppressed a shiver, angry that he would take advantage of her out in the open. She glared down at him, but his hat obscured his face.

"I didsh allsh I's could," the March Hare slurred before slumping forward onto the table.

The Hatter slammed his hat on the table and ran

his hand through his hair. Even though he radiated anger, his fingers were gentle as they trailed to the top of her thigh.

"We had a little drinking contest," he finally explained. "And I lost, or rather, everyone won because they are in repose and I am all alone."

Mary Ann attempted to shake his hand off, but it would not budge. "I did not serve any liquor with the tea, *sir*."

The Hatter grinned. "It's amazing what you can stumble upon in this house." He leaned back in his chair and stared up at her with his deep black eyes. "You always find something to whet your appetite."

He turned away from her, and his hand dropped from her leg. Mary Ann stepped out of his way, just as he talked the Frog-Footman into taking a drink with him. The Dormouse drunkenly raised his small paw to announce he was ready for another, and Mary Ann left them alone to suffer the Hatter's demons.

* * *

Mary Ann went outside to clear her head. She could hear the Frog-Footman drunkenly singing and the bang and clatter of pots and pans being scrubbed by the other servants. The White Rabbit never came to the party, and Mary Ann was slightly worried. Though he was always late, he always at least made an appearance.

She folded her arms against the night's chill. Something was not right, and had never been ever since she had decided the Hatter was not mad. She had always thought the Red Queen was the one who enjoyed chess, but she was beginning to realize more and more that everyone was just a pawn of the Hatter.

Which made her wonder: what move would he make next? And would she lose the game?

The house had gone eerily silent, and she knew from the darkness in the dining room window that the Hatter's guests had been sent away. Mary Ann trudged through the servants' door to find that the kitchen was empty. She shoved up her sleeves, glad for the quiet, and settled into scrubbing a large pan. The task was joyfully meaningless and allowed her to forget the night's events, the touch of the Hatter's fingers on her skin.

"Why do you believe I'm not mad, Mary Ann?"

Her fingertips skimmed soapy water as the Hatter's voice drifted in from the doorway. She was lost in the heat of his voice but shook herself from it and returned to scrubbing.

"It sounds like nonsense, but you mean what you say," she explained.

"Say what you mean, Mary Ann."

She turned, exasperated, and he grinned at her. He was a large and looming shadow. She did not want him to come any closer.

"A tornado is similar," she said and gripped the edges of the table as he strode closer. "It seems like it has no direction, but it knows where it's headed."

"A tornado?" he mused. The candles flickered as he moved into the room. She willed herself not to run. She held her breath as he walked around the table. He shrugged out of his torn dinner jacket. He tossed it on the table, now only in his dress shirt. It clung to his well-muscled upper body, which he kept so well hidden. He rolled up his wrinkled cuffs, and she stared at his pale forearms. When he looked at her, his eyes were bright and the scar by his eye was red.

He was the most beautiful man she had ever seen.

"If I'm a tornado, aren't you afraid of the danger?"

"I was never under the impression that you wanted me." She swallowed. "In danger."

"Oh, but I do," he said. He was in front of her now; she could smell rain and the heat of his skin. A lock of jet-black hair fell next to his eye as he caged her between his arms. Her fingers dug into the counter as he leaned down and pressed his lips against her neck. Her pulse fluttered in immediate response, and she ignored the urge to let her eyes slide shut.

"I have felt that for quite some time." His words made patterns on her skin. "Even though I shouldn't. Because you are a widow, with a child. And I am a madman." His mouth ran up her neck again, and he licked her pulse.

She released her hold on the counter and pressed her hands against his chest. His shirt was paper-thin, and she could feel his heart beating. She itched to touch him, skin to skin, but she tucked her head away from his lips, so that he was only breathing in her ear.

"I can't do this," she said.

"Why?" he whispered. "Are you jealous?"

"Of what?"

"Figs."

She glanced up at him. "Excuse me?"

"*Figs*, Mary Ann."

She shook her head slowly. "That makes no sense."

"Like your jealousy," he murmured. "Your fear." He set his lips to her forehead. "You taste like fear."

"Fear doesn't have a taste."

"Neither does regret, but you taste like that as well." He nipped at her ear. "You haven't asked me where the servants are."

She said nothing, even as she felt him untie her apron. He tossed it next to his jacket and then pulled on the shoulders of her gown, until it gaped and revealed the breadth of skin above her breasts.

"I sent them away," he said.

"When?"

"At midnight."

"I thought it was always midnight."

He stared down at her. "You're too smart for me."

She looked into his fathomless eyes and searched for an answer. "Who are you trying to trick?"

He shook his head. "You're not part of that game, Mary Ann. You're for treats." He cocked his head. "What will it be, my little foundling?"

The house was silent, save for their breathing, and she noticed the color high in his cheeks, as if he were feverish. She reached up and ran the pads of her fingers over his scar. His eyes fluttered shut in response to her touch, and he leaned into her hand, then pressed his lips against her palm.

She brought her hand away, and his eyes opened. He watched as she tugged her dress down and revealed her breasts to his gaze. She leaned up and pressed her lips against his, and it was fire.

He pulled her away from the counter and sat her on the table, on top of his discarded jacket. The cold air had made her nipples hard, and he took one in his mouth as he plucked the other with his fingertips. She gasped soundlessly and clutched the thick, black strands of his hair. Her husband had never touched her in such a way. He was kind, but cursory in their lovemaking. It had been nothing like this storm of passion. She ran her hands down the Hatter's strong back as his hands dropped to her thighs and parted them.

"Is this wrong, Mary Ann?" His voice was in her ear.

"Yes," she murmured. "But I don't want you to stop."

The table was set low, so that when he stepped between her thighs, there was nothing but fabric between them. She arched closer, wanting his full touch. He gave it to her, wrapping her legs around his hips. They kissed and she groaned into his mouth as he started a slow, maddening grind against her center. A spasm broke low in her belly, and she wrapped her arms tightly around him, wanting the release only he could provide.

He broke the kiss and stepped away from her, and she almost cried out in abandonment. He tore at the buttons of his shirt, revealing fine muscles and skin like alabaster. Her fingers itched to touch him, and when he came back to her, she ran her hands down his chest, scraping lightly with her nails. She leaned forward and licked his nipples. He growled, so primal and raw, and she was immediately wet.

She dropped her hands to the fall of his trousers,

and peeled the fabric away. She ran her fingers slowly down his erect cock, and she watched as he threw his head back, the tendons in his neck flexing. He set one hand on the table by her thigh as she worked him, and she felt his other hand travel up her skirts, until he delved into her center, with one finger, and then two. He stretched her, readied her, pleasured her so completely that she squeezed his cock and moaned in abandoned delight. She was lost in a tide of pleasure, and losing her perch on the table, and so he pulled her hands away from him and wrapped her legs around him again, his cock pressed at her entrance.

He thrust deeply into her, and she cried out, her fingers digging into his skin. He teased her with his thrusts, pushing deep, then shallow, then deep again, until she begged him for release. His hand went to where they were joined, and he touched her, flicking her clit so that she shattered immediately, her muscles contracting around him and bringing him to his own intense orgasm.

She was wrapped so closely around him she felt as if they were truly one, and both of their hearts beat out the same pattern so that she truly believed it.

"I've dreamed of this," he finally said, his lips at the curve of her neck. "I've dreamed of it so long I can't believe I'm awake."

She shut her eyes. "It has to remain a dream."

He released a shuddering sigh and pulled her gently off the table. He straightened and fastened their clothes. She was weak on her feet and could do nothing but sway when he found a wet rag and wiped the tears from her face. She watched as he slipped back into his jacket and grasped the folds of her apron. He walked over to her and placed the apron in one of her hands before wrapping her back in his arms. His lips met hers once more, but this time there was no gentleness. It was fierce and possessive, a pleasure-pain kiss that made it all the more bittersweet.

When it ended, his hands were clasped in her hair, and she had no choice but to look into his eyes and commit to what she had done.

"What do you want from me?" she asked wearily.

"What you want from me," he replied evenly. "We have more in common than you think, Mary Ann." He tipped his head, and the candlelight played against the contours of his face. "We have both lost people we once loved. The sorrow connects us."

"Who have you lost?"

He moved away from her, and glanced down the dim hall. "I have to put out the lights," he murmured. He glanced back at her. "Don't wander."

"Wait," she said.

He paused in the alcove, the same place where she had seen him kiss the White Knight.

"What about him?" Mary Ann asked. "What about the White Knight?"

The Hatter smiled grimly. "There is no longer anything about him. He's dead."

Mary Ann was so shocked she simply stared at the dirt floor. It was only when she could no longer hear the Hatter's tread upon the stairs that she turned and fled into the night.

* * *

Mary Ann searched for a lost pair of the White Rabbit's gloves in a grove of mulberry bushes. She hummed a lullaby her daughter had recently sung to her, and barely noticed the black carriage that halted on the road. She stood up and stretched her back as the carriage's ornate door opened and she spied the shadow of the Mad Hatter's top hat.

Mary Ann stepped gingerly out of the bush. She had avoided the Hatter and his house since the night in the kitchen. It was easier than she had thought: the White Knight's death was announced as a victorious execution by the Queen of Hearts, and it wasn't long after that the Mad Hatter had boarded up his house and abandoned his tea party table to the weeds.

But if he was suffering, he did not look it, for when Mary Ann glanced inside the carriage, he was perched inside, smiling with his top had askew.

"Mary Ann," he greeted her. "This is the second time I've seen you with weeds in your hair."

She ignored his comment, as well as the rapid beating of her heart and the sudden dampness of her palms.

"What are you doing here?"

"What *aren't* I doing? For I am doing many things." He tapped the seat next to him. "Come in and I will take you down the road."

Mary Ann glanced back at the bushes. "Not very far, I hope."

"As far as a dog's beak," he promised.

She stepped into the carriage, and when she grasped his hand, she noted he was wearing gloves. She positioned herself on the opposite seat and noticed he was dressed quite well, in a suit that actually fit him properly.

"I don't trust you," she said.

He smiled again. "I don't trust myself."

He shut the door and tapped the carriage's roof, signaling it to sputter forward on the rocky terrain. Mary Ann had never been in a carriage, but she knew this was a unique one. The ceiling was high, and from it hung rich tapestries in shades of red. The seats were large and smelled of rich leather, and for a moment she forgot her daily chores and sank into luxury.

The Mad Hatter noted her pleasure and grinned.

"So here we are," he said. "Two hedgehogs in a barrel."

Mary Ann picked the grass off her apron. "I was sorry to hear about the White Knight."

"Sorrier to see it," the Hatter replied. "I'm sure it was damn bloody." He stared out the window. "But it's known that the Queen has a thirst for blood. It's why she's engaged so long in the war your husband died for."

"Let's not talk about that," she snapped.

"Exactly!" The Hatter clapped his hands together in mocking joy.

He settled back in his seat and studied her out of hooded eyes. "Do you think about our night together, Mary Ann?"

He stood, despite the rocking of the carriage, and hooked his hands through the carriage's elaborate hangings. "Well?" he prodded, slipping his fingers through the fabric, which looked as soft as silk. "Do you?"

Her hands fisted in her lap. "It was a mistake."

"Ah," he sighed and dropped down next to her, elegant and disheveled. "Another regret." He rested his chin on his hand and surveyed her. "You have a mountain of them. It must be difficult to climb."

"What does it matter?" she bit out.

"It matters very much," he said quietly. He ran a finger down her cheek, and she shivered, relishing his touch.

"I would like to see you happy."

"I was," she admitted.

He pulled her lightly against him, her back resting against his chest. He smelled of cardamom and rainwater. She pressed her cheek against his chest as his hands ran up and down her arms. As his fingers ran up and down her flesh, she grew feverish and shifted restlessly. She wanted more of his touch but did not know how to ask.

"Will you show me?" he whispered into her ear.

"Show you?"

"What I did to make you happy."

"You touched me."

"Where?"

She placed her hand on her breast. "Here," she said and then, undaunted, squeezed the flesh. She gasped as the feeling shot down between her legs. The Hatter's hand covered hers, and he guided her fingers around her nipple. She bit back a moan and pushed her backside up against him. Her eyes widened when she felt his erection, and her head fell back on his shoulder, her neck bare for his lips.

"And then?" he whispered.

She moved her other hand down to her waist, and then lower, until she clutched the fabric between her legs. But it did not ease her torment, and she moaned her frustration. She rocked back against his hard cock, and he growled, nipping her neck as he yanked up her skirts. The air cooled her momentarily as he hooked her leg over his.

"Touch yourself," he said. He brought her hand to her bare thigh. She ran her fingers up the smooth skin, enjoying the soft touch, enjoying being cradled by this man as he coaxed her to her own pleasure.

She found her center, and she was wet. She stroked herself, moaning, until his fingers found hers again, and he placed them where she wanted, where she needed to be touched.

"Yes," he said, his voice hoarse. "Right there."

His arm went around her waist and cinched her close. She began to rock back and forth, her moans growing louder as she touched herself and rubbed against him. Her other hand traveled back to her breast, pinching her nipple, the fabric scraping against her skin. The pressure between her legs built and built, until she sobbed for release, and he gave it to her, turning her face to his and taking her mouth in a deep kiss. When he took her tongue in his mouth and sucked, it pushed her over the edge and she exploded in a fiery blaze. He drank it in through their kiss as her body shuddered against his.

When she was calm again, he pulled her dress down and took her hand from between her legs. She watched as he licked her fingers clean. His eyes were dark and steady on hers, conveying what words could not.

* * *

She fell asleep. When she woke, she was still cradled in his arms. She rubbed her eyes and noticed the carriage was no longer moving. Darkness blanketed the interior. She peered out the window in dismay.

"Where are we?"

He shifted, his arms falling away from her. She shivered, suddenly very cold.

"The Court of Hearts," he said.

She shoved away from him and stood among the flowing tapestries. She recognized them, then, as the Queen's own colors. He had planned it all.

"You said you were only going up the road," she said furiously.

"I did." He smiled, but it did not reach his eyes. "But I did not say how far."

She stomped her foot childishly. "Why are we here?"

He looked away from her. "So I can turn myself in."

"No!"

"Yes."

"You're mad," she said.

He smiled again. "If only, my little foundling."

She wanted to throw something at him, but she could only twist her fingers in her dress. "Why are you doing this?"

"Why do we do anything, my pet? It's all only for the one chance to make us happy."

"How will turning yourself in make you happy?"

140

He sighed. The night had painted shadows under his eyes. "A baker cannot make a cake without flour, Mary Ann." He pursed his lips. "What sort of life is it for me, hiding behind half truths? My lover died because of it. And any sort of life with you is like a wickless candle. The flame is out before it is even lit."

"That's not true," she said bitterly.

He looked up at her, his hands folded in front of him. There was no laughter in his eyes, and she knew he had decided this path long ago. "Your daughter," he said patiently, "deserves better."

She ducked her head as the tears threatened to fall.

"Let me go, Mary Ann. I will plead my case. I will sing my song." He stood and rested his hands on her shoulders. "Will you wait for me?"

Her own hands traveled up, and linked around his wrists. "I've waited for you all my life. What is an hour or two more?"

He pressed his lips to her forehead, and his hand caught hers, lacing their fingers together. He released her, and she watched as he opened the carriage door and leaped into the night, toward the sharp spiral towers of the Court of Hearts.

After the tears had dried, she opened her hand. He had left her with a piece of angel's trumpet, the color of a glorious sunset. She ran her fingers over the delicate folds and threaded it through her hair.

A Perfect Creature

Bernie Mojzes

It is not the Rabbit's frantic and hurried thrusts that she misses most, nor the Cat's sandpaper tongue.

Alice cups her hands over her breasts, pulling at them one by one until they pop out of the suctioning curve of her palm; pulls at her belly, and at the flesh of her thighs and arms the same way. Grip, pull, release. Her pelvis arches involuntarily, and she lets one finger slip between moist lips to press against her clit. She closes her eyes and bites the inside of her lip.

It is not the Hatter's incoherent monologue as he fills her mouth that pervades her dreams, or the Red Queen's waxy paper folds, tasting faintly of the memory of honey, and of bees. Not the Dormouse's tender but ultimately unsatisfying attentions. Not even the Walrus's blunted tusk probing deep, deeper than anything before or since or ever would be, pressed against and pushed through her cervix as his whiskers tickled her thighs. Not the thrill of that sudden realization: *He might kill me.* He almost had.

She turns on her side so she can better reach behind her, slipping two, then three fingers inside as deeply as she can as she tugs at her clit gently with thumb and forefinger. Remembering, she moans. It rises, feral, from somewhere deep below her throat.

Some things are better as a memory, and the thick, curved pieces of scarred ivory lay long unused in the back of her underwear drawer, next to the knife that had harvested them.

The man beside her smiles sleepily, his hand already coaxing his cock into awareness before he himself has fully found that state. "What time is it?" he asks.

It's still dark. Who cares what time it is?

Alice turns to him, reaches for him. What was his name? *Billy*. She grabs the Billy's goat, wet fingers wrapped in tender scrotal flesh, and pulls him to her, pulls him abruptly from his half sleep. His cock is long and thin, hot and hard, and it slips inside her easily. She digs fingernails into his ass and draws him in until his pelvic bone presses hard against hers, her clit rolling between them as she rocks against him. Only then does she release the breath she'd been unaware of holding. Only then does she relax and let him start fucking her with long, smooth strokes.

His cock moves in time with his body; his body in time with his cock. It feels as if his cock grows with his excitement; it very well might. But it isn't enough. It doesn't seek out all the spaces within her, doesn't twist and writhe inside her, doesn't pulse or throb, and won't until that brief moment as he finishes.

Behind her, someone stirs, roused by their fucking. She feels fingers exploring, and the cold drip of lube. He works it into her ass, and then slowly pushes himself in. He is patient, gentle, letting her relax around him, forcing nothing.

"Who's that?" Alice asks.

The man behind her pushes himself deep as he leans over her. He is wider at the base, almost too wide, though she knows that a few minutes of fucking will resolve that small issue. His mouth is near her ear. "Billy," he says.

She looks at the man in front of her. "Then who the fuck are you?"

"Dylan. I'm a friend of Billy's."

"Oh. Yeah. Pleased to meet you." She's forgotten his name already.

There's more movement in the darkness. Billy and not-Billy move in counter-rhythm, alternating pistons in her cunt and ass. Alice closes her eyes and loses herself in the rhythm.

He would do that sometimes as she lay coiled with him. For hours. One in, one out, until both spent inside her. Then, with a ripple that rolled across the whole of his body, both legs would pull free of her, and in the space of a breath, the next two would find her, plunge deep, and begin again. His other legs caressed her, suckled on her nipples, her neck. Inevitably one of the softly pulsing limbs would find her mouth, push past her lips, suctioning her tongue as she sucked its length.

Something hard touches her lips, and she parts them to accept it. Fingers grip her hair. She tastes salt and remembers the earthy flavor of fresh mushrooms. He had smelled of poppies and tasted of mushrooms, and the liquid that oozed from the pores in his pads as she sucked him had made her dizzy. Euphoric. She can feel the orgasm build inside her. She lets it take her, keeping only enough of herself aware to avoid biting down on the cock in her mouth.

At least, not *too* hard.

Her orgasm brings one of her partners along for the ride. Softening, he pulls out, and another takes his place behind her.

Now the two move in unison, Billy and... No, Billy was gone. Dan or Derrick or something, and someone else who also wasn't Billy. Not-Billy and not-Billy, moving together, filling her together. Sometimes he would do this to her as well, when she would ride his prolegs. But he would keep his body still. Only his prolegs would move, plunging in and out of her. He had less control of these false legs, the limbs that were even now withering and falling away. Oh, she would miss them! Less control, so that they always moved in unison, and less stamina. But he had four pairs, and they always gave them enough time for the rest of him to recover.

They could have fucked forever. They should have.

She should never have left, this time.

The cock in her mouth thrusts more insistently; its owner grips her hair and groans. The first spurt fills Alice's mouth. She wants the rest on her breasts.

Once, he had positioned himself over her, his face between her legs, his spinneret—which, for reasons as logical as his having a face and arms, was set at the end of his abdomen like a spider's—poised over her mouth. His tongue caressed her clit as his fingers explored her depths. His legs and prolegs pushed and prodded her, sucking her flesh all over, thighs and hips and belly and breasts and throat, bringing the blood to the surface. They rubbed against her and against each other. She had touched a tentative tongue to his spinnerets. They clutched at her, working, and when she drew back, a slender thread of silk stretched between them, clinging to her tongue. It was sweet, and she swallowed it, then pressed her face against the grasping organ. He groaned as she fucked his spinneret with fingers and tongue, and then shuddered so massively that she feared his skin might split. All of his legs ejaculated at once, hot absinthe spilling over her body, florescent cream pooling between her breasts and on her belly.

He scooped it with trembling fingers and fed it to her. She had hallucinated for hours.

Alice pulls the throbbing cock out of her mouth and aims it at her chest, but the position is all wrong. She is lying on her side, sandwiched between men, and the semen spurts hot on DanDerrickDavid's skin.

"Hey! What the fuck, Mark?" DanDerrickDavid doesn't stop fucking her. If anything, he fucks her harder.

"Shit. Sorry, Dylan."

Dylan. That was it. Alice feels a laugh bubbling in her throat. It turns him on. He probably wasn't even aware of it. She spits the rest of Mark onto Dylan's chest, then bites down on his nipple, hard. He stiffens and clutches at her, and she pulls him from between her legs, jerking him until he spills over his own belly and chest, and the side of her face. She runs her tongue over his skin, taking some of his seed into her mouth, and some of Mark's, then kisses him deeply. He hesitates, then returns the kiss with fire.

"I think I like you, Dan," she says. "You should come more often."

"Dylan," he says.

Alice pulls at his lip with her teeth. "Eat me," she says.

She pushes back until whoever is behind her is lying on his back, his cock in her ass. Dylan positions himself between both of their legs and does as he is told. His tongue traces her labia as he slips two fingers inside her. He pulls her clit between his lips, nips it gently with his teeth as he sucks it into his mouth. Just right.

She hopes he'll stick around for a while, at least until she finds her way back.

God, why had she left? Why had she let him send her away? In the beginning, it had been difficult, so many legs, so many limbs, so many... But she had been strong, persevered. And the lazy smoke he'd shared with her soothed the overused flesh. Together, they had found that place beyond pleasure, beyond pain, beyond ecstasy. A place of flesh and euphoria.

And each time she had helped him molt—peeled the stiff, cracked shell from his body to reveal the tender, sensitive new skin—he was bigger. All of him. Eighteen new, fresh, larger limbs to explore her, wriggling deeper into her cunt and ass, pushing deeper into her throat.

A pair of legs straddle her face, and a hard cock pushes past her lips. Eric. She knows his shape and taste, knows the motion of his hips. She tilts her head back and relaxes into it.

Someone pours oil between her breasts, spreads it with his hands and penis. There was another? She can't see past Eric's balls. She can hear Billy snoring. Okay, there's another, and he rubs his cock between her breasts. She presses them together, enfolding him, and gives herself to the motion. A cock in her mouth, and in her ass, and rubbing against her body, all at once. A tongue on her clit and fingers in her cunt.

It would have to do. Until she finds her way back. Until she finds the rabbit hole, the door, the looking glass.

Somewhere, the one she needs is waiting for her, warm in his silken blanket tight against the rough bark of a tree. He had already started spinning when he told her to leave. Alice had thought it looked comfortable. She had thought it was for her.

It *was* for her. He just didn't know it. But he would, when she returned.

She's done it before. There is always a way back. Always.

It's building. DylanEricMarkBilly moves inside her and over her. He fucks her throat and her tits. He grasps her hips and pulls her ass down hard on his cock. He's tonguing her hole and frigging her clit fast with his thumb.

She will find her way back. When dawn comes, she'll leave her boys in their exhausted, inefficient heaps, she'll wash them from her skin and she will find the rabbit hole. She will find it and crawl in and down and through. Yes. She will find it, and she will find him. Yes. Her body arches.

DylanEricMarkBilly makes a sound in his throat, thrusts hard against her breastbone. His cum splashes against her chin, fills the hollow of her throat.

He will be there, safe in his cocoon. Safe in silk.

It is a chain reaction. The sight of his cum spilled

over her throat makes DylanEricMarkBilly tense and gasp. He grips the back of her head in one hand, cups her cum-slick jaw with the other and thrusts deep and hard. He shudders. *Drink me.* And she does.

She will find him. She will part the silk and climb inside, into the warmth of his arms and legs, into the warmth of his silk. He will enfold her. He will find his way inside her.

DylanEricMarkBilly spends himself inside her as his tongue brings her shuddering to momentary oblivion. Together.

Together.

Coiled in his chrysalis, he will be inside her, in her mouth, her cunt, her ass. Together. The mouth that kisses hers is sweet with her fluids. His cock presses into her, and she welcomes him. Together. He fucks her fast. She's surrounded by his flesh, hot and hard, or spent and softening. They move together.

God.

They move faster.

The flesh entwined. She will find him, and join him. And as he changes, so will she. Him inside her. Her inside him.

Fuck.

They will grow. Together. Entwined. Joined. Merged. One perfect creature.

Fuck, yes!

One perfect fucking creature. Forever. Fucking. Forever...

Fuck!

Yes.

Midway Rides
Alex Picchetti

Annette shook herself. She had been staring at the cover page of an essay for the last five minutes, and she wasn't even certain what she had been contemplating. Certainly not *The Merry Wives of Windsor* or any freshman's opinion on it. She glanced at her watch: six thirty already. She sank lower into her chair, picked up the phone and dialed home.

"Hi, Pete. No, the essays are still giving me trouble. You should eat." She twirled her pen absentmindedly. "Yes. Okay. Love you too. See you tonight."

She felt guilty as she rested the phone back in its cradle. The truth was that she could have worked on her marking from home, spent the evening in the company of her husband, eaten dinner across from him, made mindless small talk about their respective days. But after yesterday's meal, she couldn't face him.

She had become totally absorbed with her dinner in a childlike way, pushing around the mashed potatoes with her fork.

"Something wrong, dear?" he had asked.

Jolted from her reverie, she had said, thoughtlessly, "I was just thinking of the letter *P*. Potatoes, parsnip, pork, plate. All of them... plain."

"But not Peter, I hope, ha-ha," he had said.

It was the "ha-ha" that had bothered her the most. Oh, she had laughed and reassured him, and that was the end of it. How embarrassing, though, to have come out and said something like that! Where had her head gone to?

But the "ha-ha" stayed with her. He had said it just like that, not a real laugh at all. Was that how he laughed? She had tried to remember, all night. She couldn't come up with another instance to compare against.

And while she had comforted him, she realized that no, in fact, Peter was just as plain and pale and pasty as the potatoes had been.

The guilt from that thought had been enough to occupy her until well past three a.m. with silent self-recriminations, and she had barely been able to face him the next morning.

So now she hid in her cramped little office, pretending she was totally absorbed with the inane, half-plagiarized papers piled on her desk so that she didn't have to worry about further Freudian slips at dinner.

She picked up her pen and began to mark.

It was eleven o'clock before she put it down again, her eyes aching and her spine popping as she stretched. The streetlights outside cast an orange glow over everything, giving the campus a strange, surreal feel. She could hear the soft echo of a thumping bass line from the residences. At least someone was having a good night.

She packed up her bags and headed for the subway. The weather was still pleasant—a slight cool touch to the air, but warm enough that she walked slowly. At this time of night there was no one in the area of the campus. Besides, if she were lucky, Peter would already be asleep by the time she reached home.

The subway itself was practically empty at this time of night, all of the clubgoers already out, and empty of her fellow commuters. Only an older, white-bearded gentleman in a vest and a small woman with a flower in her hair shared the train. The gentle rocking of the car as it began its trek made her realize how sleepy she was. Normally the idea of closing her eyes here would have been unthinkable, but how dangerous could these people possibly be?

She awoke in total darkness.

She grabbed at her purse—had she been abducted? But no, the seats of the subway were still beneath her, and her purse was closed and on her lap. Had the train broken down? Her eyes began to adjust. Outside the car, she could see faint bobbing lights. The train doors were slightly ajar.

"Did we break down?" she asked, and when no one answered, she carefully groped her way to the exit of the train. Along the cavern, people with lights— *Cell phones?* she wondered—made their way, seemingly unperturbed by the strangeness of the situation.

The portly grandfather who had shared her cabin went past her at a dead run. "Wait!" she shouted after him. He was spry! She tried to chase him, but even her short heels made things difficult. "What happened?"

No answer; he was too far ahead to hear. She tried to catch up to the others, struggling with her shoes on the gravelly floor of the tunnels. "Where are we going? Is there a leak? Is someone coming to get us? Where are the conductors?"

The lights faded around a corner. Fear gripped her, but she pressed on.

A carnival greeted her as she rounded the bend.

Unperturbed by the tracks running through it, it filled every inch of the tunnel with balloons and flags and games and rides. Music cantered forth with the force of a physical being, followed by the smell of candyfloss and beer nuts. How had she not heard it? How had she not smelled it?

She wandered between the garishly decorated stalls, the barkers' voices surrounding her. There was something odd about the toy prizes, but she couldn't quite put her finger on what it was. And all the attractions called for tickets, but the slots for them were almost as wide across as her hand—and there wasn't a ticket vendor in sight.

"This is impossible!" she exclaimed.

"But here it is," someone said.

She searched for the source of the voice. It seemed to have come from a small, dark tent, almost recessed into the wall, overshadowed by the bright lights and glitz of the rest of the festival. But there was no one there.

"Come inside," said the voice, this time directly behind her. She jumped. The man—jowly, rotund, and squinting—hustled her toward the open flap of the tent. *Tarot Readings—Price Negotiable*, the sign at the door read.

"Oh no, I couldn't," she demurred, but she was already on the soft seat, surrounded by a gentle haze of incense, the flap dropping down behind her. Little lights flared up near the top of the tent, giving only a shadowy illumination to the table she sat at. At the same time, several bottles of various shapes and sizes standing on rickety shelves seemed to glow from within, wisps of smoke floating out of each.

"What do you prefer?" said the man, picking out a few after a moment's consideration. "Bark of the shisha tree?" He waved it under her nose. "Fruit of the lulava flower?" A second bottle. "Ghelyoon seed extract?" Another.

Annette held her head. "They all smell so—strange," she said.

"Of course they don't," he said. "Only to those who have never smelled them before."

"I've never even heard of them!"

"Well, whose fault is that?" he said irritably. "Not mine, I imagine." He shook his head. "Never mind, I shall choose." And he picked a little green bottle and tipped it out onto the table.

"Oh, don't, you'll set the tablecloth on fire—" But the flame dribbled out into a bowl she hadn't seen and lit up the table, and now she could see a pack of cards at his seat, and these he began to shuffle.

"Once," he said, the ruffling of the cards punctuating his words, "I would have asked you to pick a card to represent yourself." *Brrrrp.* "But I have found that no one ever knows themselves correctly, so it is best to let the cards decide." *Shhhht.* "They, at least, know what they are." He fanned the cards out before her expectantly.

"May I ask—?"

"No." He gave her a severe look. "We can discuss payment after you have finished here."

This seemed fundamentally backward to Annette, but she was disinclined to argue with a man so pinched that she feared his face would fall in on itself. She chose a card.

"The Hanged One." He twirled the card in his fingers and looked pensively into the light. One minute passed, then two. Annette shifted uncomfortably and was about to leave when he said, "It could be a number of things. But for *you*: passively waiting, giving up."

"What is that supposed to mean?"

"Exactly what I said and nothing more." He tapped the card against the table. "There are lessons left to learn, and they will require sacrifices. But they will give insight. Do you want that, or do you want to remain stagnant?" He looked directly at her—or into her, she felt, boring through and finding a lack she didn't want to acknowledge.

"But of course *you* can't answer that, being who you are." He snorted and pushed the card across the table to her. "Take this to the twins in the fun house. They will know what to do." He stood up and opened the curtain.

"Thank you," she said, not certain what she was thanking him for at all.

"And I am *not* rude," he called after her as she hurried toward the midway. "I am direct and correct, and you are not. That is all." She shrank down and walked faster, ashamed of her own thoughts. But how had he known them?

Her stomach growled, and she realized it was nearly midnight, and she hadn't eaten a thing since lunch. She bought a corn dog and, on a whim, a green sno-cone and ate them as she walked.

The fun house was an enormous thing, filling the tunnel at the very back of the carnival. It seemed to Annette that the only way to get past the blockade was through the back of the house, but as she took the steps up to the hot pink porch, she felt fearful. What was beyond the carnival? What if it was nothing but more darkness?

The porch was dark, and the front door was locked when she tried it. She rattled the handle and knocked, but there was no response from inside.

"You have to give it your ticket."

She whirled around. "I wish people would stop sneaking up on me!" she snapped.

The light of a cigar bobbed toward her, the light slowly revealing a grin and eyes, and then the rest of the man who had been lurking in the shadows. "Who's sneaking?" he asked. "You walked right on by, never even stopped to notice me." He closed the space between them suddenly, and she backed up against the door. "Gotcher ticket?"

"All I have is this," she mumbled, pushing the tarot card between them.

He grinned as he took it from her. "Well that's a mighty fine likeness, don'tcha think?"

She shook her head, and he handed her back the card. As she stared at it in the half-light available, a shiver ran through her: the Hanged One was her, practical suit and all, tied upside down to a T-cross.

The carny took the card back from her and slipped it into a slot near the door lock.

Multicolored lightbulbs flashed like paparazzi cameras and organ music began to blare. Deafened and half-blind, Annette stumbled through a doorway she hadn't seen open into a dazzlingly lit hall of mirrors.

"Have fun, love!" called the carny, blowing a kiss, and he shut the door behind her.

The mirrors made her reflection dance down the hall, darting up to be as tall as a tree or shrinking to the size of a munchkin, and as she made her way along, she couldn't help but laugh at some of the twisty-turny contortions her reflection got into.

"Glad you enjoy it," one of her reflections said, and she shrieked.

The mirror spun around lazily, picking up speed with a soft whirring noise until it spat forth a gentleman dressed in an elegant purple suit and a crushed velvet top hat. He caught on to her for support and sent them both spinning down the hall, crashing her up against the window at the end to finally stop.

"My apologies, my dear," he said, his breath soft against her cheek. He pulled back abruptly, sweeping into an elaborate bow. "Welcome to my carnival."

"What is this place?" she asked. "How did it get here?"

"A magician never reveals his secrets," he chastised her. He looked around, then conspiratorially leaned in to her. "However, I'm not a very good magician at all. I can be persuaded in, oh, so many numbers of ways! I've quite lost count." He straightened. "But! Before I go trusting you with that, do *you* trust *me*, I wonder?"

"I—" she began to say, but stopped as he produced a long, white scarf from nowhere. She applauded politely and he tipped his hat. "Well, you see, how can I trust you? I don't know you."

"Ah, but you trust all sorts of people you don't know," he said cheerfully.

"Do I?"

"You trust the token-taker on the subway to let you in with a pass, and the store clerk to give you proper change. And then the people you do know: you trust your husband to be faithful and your friends to remember your birthday. All sorts of little trusts, all the time. But let me ask you something else. Do you trust anyone with the big things?"

"I don't have any big things," she said demurely.

"Then you don't have anything at all!" he cried. "Will you let me give you a gift of one such thing?"

"Oh, no, I couldn't accept a gift from you."

"But you've already taken one to be here, and given it back to the carnival. Let me replace it for you." He held up the scarf, pinched in two fingers of each hand. "Do you trust me?"

"I suppose I must, if you put it that way," she said, a little smile on her lips.

He began to wrap the linen around her eyes. "Think of it as a magic trick," he said. "A transformation, if you will."

"But how will I see it?"

"Do you trust me?" he asked again, tightening the blindfold. She could see nothing.

"I do. But I was told to find the twins."

She felt two sets of hands take her arms on either side. "They are my assistants. They will be with you throughout my trick." He patted her cheek. "And if you want to go, just tell them, 'This isn't fun anymore.' Can you do that?"

"I think so."

He made her demonstrate. When he was satisfied, he announced, "Wonderful. Then let the magic begin!"

The hands on her arms tightened, one on each side holding her hand and gripping her bicep.

Then the floor gave way.

She tumbled through the air for what felt like hours, screaming as she went.

She yelped when she bounced, still airborne, and giggling arose from either side of her. The hands slipped down her arms, lowering her to the floor. Her heart pounded, and her ears rushed with sound, almost drowning out the soft thumps to her left and right.

"Come, come." The voices were androgynous, and age was impossible to tell. She began to wonder if she had been taken by faeries.

The hands took hold of her again, pulling her gently left and right, spinning her around slowly. Her hair brushed against her cheek and swept against the small of her back. "Come, come."

She panted in response. Her voice had quite left her. Where did they want her to go? Every part of her body felt flush and awake.

159

The left one slid a single finger up her arm, over the silk of her blouse. It caught occasionally on the dampness of her skin, and she shivered. The one on the right followed suit, tracing a river along the underside of her arm, then slowly back down. They drew spirals in the palms of her hands and ran their fingers along the edges of her fingers. She pulled away, then gave her hands back. It almost—but not quite—tickled. It was the strangest sensation.

As her heartbeat calmed, she became aware of a slow, pulsating beat that filled her body and brought its rhythm into an exact time. She could hear, beyond the walls of the fun house, the tinny carnival music keeping its own time, but in here, she only had the percussive beat and the odd sensations running over her hands.

She realized that with each of their other hands, the twins had begun pushing her waist back and forth between them, swaying her in time with the music. She relaxed into it, marveling—she had never had much grace, and yet this felt perfectly right.

Their hands glided up her arms again, this time one flowing down her back and the other lightly brushing down her front. She gasped as the silk shifted against the small of her back and slid against the cotton of her bra. She felt dizzy.

"It's..." She swallowed. Her mouth was so dry.

"Would you like something to drink?" The one in front asked.

She nodded. The one behind her took charge of things, continuing to sway her as its fingers danced along the curve of her waist. Moments later, the second twin returned—she realized she could tell where they were by the change in the air around her— and something soft and wet slid across her lips.

She opened her mouth to it immediately, without thinking, suckling on the finger presented to her obediently. A licorice taste filled her mouth, bright and sharp; it was ice-cold too. Not at all like the allsorts she liked to buy. Intense.

The finger withdrew and returned twice more.

"Better?"

She nodded. "What was that?"

"The leftover syrup and ice from your sno-cone."

"I didn't realize it tasted like—that," she said wonderingly. "I thought I ordered the green one."

The one behind her asked, "What did you think absinthe tasted like?"

But before she could answer, they had taken her firmly again and began dancing in earnest.

Now hands slid down her legs over her pantyhose—she couldn't keep track anymore of who was where—bringing her leg up and forcing her to balance on her toes, spinning her in place, moving her like their personal ballerina doll. The music grew louder as they whisked her through the steps, and she let herself go limp in their arms, flung to and fro in a frenzy of music until one suddenly swung her into a dip, then slowly—so tantalizingly slowly—lowered her to the floor.

A warm draft spun around her body in lazy eddies, and the floor beneath her back was covered in a soft fur rug, and her head was surrounded by soft pillows. She shifted against them, feeling the exquisite softness of them against her shoulders, and the ticklish feeling of the fur.

She dimly became aware that she felt naked. But unlike other times, she didn't feel exposed. The blindfold, wrapped around her eyes, was a comforting pressure.

She felt something soft and sticky pressed against her lips, and she parted them to allow the item—some sort of delicious candy—into her mouth. She rolled it slowly with her tongue. The hard shell dissolved away to reveal a cake-like center. When she swallowed, a finger brought more absinthe to her mouth, and she indulged happily.

Gently, the twins rolled her onto her front, propping her up on pillows before beginning their gentle mirrored tracing, this time starting at her fingertips but moving up her arms and all the way down her back; over her buttocks, which she clenched from ticklishness, and down the backs of her thighs. She realized just how sore she was; sitting at a desk all day had left her back stiff, and her shoes, while practical, did little to keep her calves and ankles from aching.

As one they massaged her, each working ever deeper into her muscles until she almost felt as though they were part of her. She noticed there wasn't much sound here at all; the distant music seemed farther away, and there was no sound of clothes shifting. She wondered if the twins were naked, idly wondering what they looked like. They were so quiet that she couldn't hear them over her own breathing. The pillows were filled with flower petals; a pleasant scent of roses and lavender surrounded her.

Each shift of her body rubbed her against the rug, and by the end her nipples were so sensitive that she almost asked them to stop. Once or twice, when they massaged her hips and ass, the fur brushed against her clitoris and caught in her pubic hair in an embarrassingly arousing way.

They began to bind her arms, one in a strange clingy material she thought might be saran wrap, the other in something oddly rough and yet smooth, and the smell reminded her of her grandfather. Leathery. Around her legs they wound a soft rope, binding them together. It felt comforting.

The hands rolled her back over, stroking her bare breasts and the curve of her stomach. One of them gently began to comb her hair, the feathery strands of it falling over her body. When they finished, a luxuriously soft jersey sheet was drawn up over her.

She did not hear them leave, for she was fast asleep.

When she awoke, she was surprised to realize she was clothed. There was no blindfold on her eyes. A dream. She could not even bring herself to admit it was a very *pleasant* dream. Even thinking about it brought a blush to her cheeks.

And yet, she was still in the fun house. A door was cut in the wall at the head of the room, and another to the foot of her bed—that must have been where they had brought her in. Had she really imagined the whole thing? A hallucination from the alcohol, perhaps?

The jersey sheet, the scented pillow, the fur rug all promised that it had been true.

And her pantyhose were missing.

She burned with shame. Rather than finding her way home, here she was, playing strange games. A thought occurred to her suddenly, and she rushed to her purse to ensure nothing had been taken. Instead of her wallet she found more cards—one emblazoned with the number fourteen, sporting two faceless cherubs pouring a green liquid between cups; and another, XVII, of her sailing naked through the air. She tucked them back in, not sure what to do with them, and pushed through the door at the head of the room.

Promptly she found herself back in the vibrant lights and cacophonous music of the midway. Everything was brighter now! Her eyes saw things more sharply, noticed things she hadn't before—such as the sno-cone vendor's cart, with the green clearly marked ABSINTHE. The others were LIMONCELLO, GRAND MARNIER and CHERRY CORDIAL. She blushed.

And there, just past the stand, was the man in the hat.

"So?" he said as she approached. "Was it magical?" That devilish little grin again. She felt fluttery and a little ill.

"A trick, more like," she said a little severely.

"I didn't hear the magic words," he said with false contrition. He slid an arm around her waist. "Was it not fun?"

"It... wasn't what I expected," she said.

"What magician worth his salt would ever give you what you expected?"

She couldn't answer that.

"But it seems it worked. You're seeing more clearly, aren't you? Come on," he said, his fingers playing up her spine like a piano. "There's a whole midway for us to explore."

He took her into a huge tent entitled FREAKSHOW. Giant glass chambers filled the space, each with carnies in a tableau. They were all painted gray or taupe. There was a couple lying on a bed, rigidly next to each other, not touching, not looking at each other; the bed was made up of long, thin nails. A contortionist, wedged between giant wood blocks with titles like *parents*, *work*, *children*, *spouse* was wrapped around himself so tightly that she wondered if he could breathe. A series of acrobats in a mockup of a subway train, dangling by one arm wrapped in cloth a full foot above the floor, seemingly unperturbed by the strain on their bodies, their faces blank and colorless. A "carpenter" worked his way up two poles utterly unsupported by horizontal steps, a sling of bricks over his shoulder, only to have the poles slapped out from under him by the foreman and be forced to start over in his Sisyphean ordeal. The scenes went on as far as she could see.

The magician pressed her into a space between the married couple's box and a tightrope walker attempting to balance as weights dropped on one side of her pole—debts, debts, more debts, piling higher as she teetered to one side.

"Awful, isn't it?" he said, pressing her against the cold metal of the railing. "No one should live like this, and yet so many do." His nose grazed her cheek, one hand cupping her neck, the other tugging gently on her blouse. "Quiet, uninteresting lives, without passion, with only worries to fill the days."

"But that isn't what they are," she insisted. "They're still circus performers."

The silk slipped loose of her skirt, and his fingers wound their way up her back as he toyed with her hair. "Everyone is a performer," he breathed. "And they've performed it so long that they believe it. They need to be shaken out of it." His hands dropped to the hem of her skirt, pushing it up along her legs, circling the fabric slowly as he began to kiss her neck.

She gripped the lapels of his coat to keep her balance. The stroking of the fabric brought back memories of the fun house, and his fingers winding into the band of her panties tugged against her cunt. She gasped. He shoved the offending piece of clothing down hungrily, pressing against her. When he kissed her on the mouth, she opened herself to him, responding in kind to his grinding, clutching at him, letting him claim her with his tongue. The rough texture of his pants against her only excited her further.

He plucked her bra open deftly, and she thrilled at the feeling of an experienced partner. His gloved hands gripped and pulled at the flesh on her back, transforming *that last ten pounds I need to lose* wordlessly into an erogenous zone, causing fire to spread through her. She explored the wiry hair on his chest, the sweat-slicked skin beneath velvet. She pulled away to fight with the buttons of his coat.

She didn't know how far she would have gone

had she not caught the tableau-husband's eye in that moment. He stared at her impassively, watching her moan, and all she could think was *Peter*.

She knocked the magician's hat away.

"Hey now," he protested, straightening.

She pushed him away, just enough to pull her panties back up, and fled.

She ran toward the Ferris wheel, ducking into the waiting tent to hide. From afar it had seemed full of happy couples, but as she came in she realized they were just paintings.

Inside were three carnies taking a smoke break.

"Now here's the girl everyone's been waiting to see," said the man. He laughed, not kindly. She could see all sorts of tattoos on each of the carnies; his were varied, but the largest was a dragon's body winding all around. She could not see a head on it. She could see faces, though; illustrations of the tarot man, the ringleader, the man with the cigar...

"She's the one that's got Hattie all agog?" One of the women flicked her ashes at Annette. She was naked from the waist up. Her back was a huge set of wings, matched only by her shockingly large breasts. "She's a mess."

"Isn't he married?" drawled the other, who wound her way behind Annette. "Scandalous." Her neck was elongated well past natural length, and her face was a mess of scars and tattooed teeth.

"Isn't it," said the first woman, stubbing out the cig. "People these days just have no morals."

"You're one to talk, Jubs," cracked the man. His mouth was full of silver teeth.

"Mmm." The woman sidled up to Annette. "But I don't pretend at modesty." She pulled at Annette's shirt, opening it the rest of the way in one swift move.

Annette backed up, but the other woman was waiting for her. She reached down and pulled free the bra that hung limply around Annette's breasts. Her nipples were erect, waiting for the touch Annette had denied them.

"Can you call this sexy? I ask you," she said mockingly.

"She *could* be, but she wilts away when she gets even the littlest bit hot," said the bird-woman.

"I just want to leave," said Annette quietly.

"*We* don't have anyone, if you want to play," said the long-necked woman. She bit Annette's ear.

"Poor June, left for a fading flower." The bird-woman sashayed, her breasts rubbing provocatively against Annette. "Bearded ladies just don't get any respect."

"Stay and play with us," the other woman said, grinding herself against Annette's ass.

"No! I want to go! This—this isn't fun anymore," she said, assertively trying the words the magician had given her.

It worked. The women sulked away to the corner, and she hated herself for her ambivalence about that. She let her hair fall forward, trying to conceal the flush on her face.

The man approached. She turned away.

"I'm just an artist, lovie," he said with a smirk. "No need to look like that. Big man with tattoos is scary, eh? Stereotyping, that is." He patted her cheek.

It was meant to be fatherly. "But you have to go up before you can go out. What's a carnival without a ride on the old wheel, eh?" He was close enough now that she could smell the rye and grease on him.

"D'you want a gift before you go?" he asked.

"No." She had had enough of gifts.

"Too bad," he said gleefully, whipping out a pen and grabbing her arm. She shrieked as he scribbled two designs on her: XV and a caricature of a man in a hat, then an eighteen. She jerked her arm away, his fingernails leaving little crescents all up her arm.

"Well, that's it for you, lovie!" he said, slapping her on the ass. "Come on, let's get you on that last ride, hey!"

He half-led, half-dragged her to the Ferris wheel, clamping her in despite her protests. Her clothing still lay on the ground as he strapped her into the machine. When he was done, he jumped on next to her, wiggling his legs into the wide-open air. Below, the women slammed the lever on.

"Have fun!" they shouted, cackling wildly as the man straddled the steel bar of Annette's carriage, seeming not to care a whit as the machine juddered to life.

"Y'see, they have to obey the rules," he told her over the noise. "I don't."

She clenched her eyes shut, but her sharpened senses felt each movement as he danced along the bar, each jolt of the metal, the drop of her stomach as they climbed higher and higher.

Then, he wasn't on the carriage anymore.

She opened her eyes, afraid he had fallen to his

death. But there he was, standing on one of the spires that held the wheel in place, his foot on the giant bolt.

"Well, lovie, you wanted to leave, but you haven't paid your dues yet!"

"What?" she cried.

"Too late now! Away we go," he shouted over the wind that had picked up in the subway tunnel.

He kicked the bolt.

The wheel groaned, the bolt spinning out with unnatural speed, its opposite number tearing under the weight of the giant machine. Annette screamed as it pitched forward, rolling through the garish lights of the carnival town, rolling toward the fun house, red-green-blue-yellow-red-green-blue-faster-faster-faster-faster...

She came to with a sickening jolt.

Still sitting in the subway car.

Her hands scrambled to confirm that she was dressed, alive, unharmed—all true. Nothing was missing. Her heart raced. She had never had a dream that vivid, or that terrifying.

Or that arousing. She was uncomfortably aware of her panties, clammy, sticking between her legs.

But it was a dream, she told herself. Only that.

She half ran home, the subway clock flashing 4:10 a.m. after her. The street seemed nearly dead, only the orange streetlights illuminating the bare concrete.

She entered the apartment quietly, hoping not to wake her husband. When she tried to sneak through the living room, shoes in hand, she found him sitting on the sofa, waiting, in the dark.

"Where were you?" he said in a low voice.

"I fell asleep."

"That's dangerous."

The tone of his voice, or the way he said his words... It didn't fit. It wasn't Peter.

She came closer.

As her eyes adjusted, she saw he was naked save for his pants, which lay half-open. He sat with his legs spread wide, taking up space, self-assured in a way that Peter was not.

She came closer.

It was Peter's face and body, more or less. But the eyes, the expression...

He grinned, and she could see the silver of his teeth. He shifted, and the dragon's body flowed over the movement of his muscles.

"You," she said quietly.

"Me," he repeated, his grin widening.

"You followed me here."

"Beat you to it, in fact."

She felt something new—rage.

"We don't take kindly to those who don't pay," he added.

"No one asked for money." She tried to remain level, but this meant the events were real. She had been trapped in some insane carnival.

"We don't do money, love." He leaned forward sharply. "We want you to give up much more than that. We want part of you."

This man had shoved her into a death trap. This man had taken her husband's body.

"Now what's it going to be, dearie?" There was a glint of metal in his hand.

She was incandescent.

"I'll tell you what," she said, approaching him slowly. He leaned back, that smug grin painted on his face. "You want something from me?"

"I could take this body," he said flippantly, patting Peter's belly.

She struck at him lightning-quick, hitting him with her shoes. He raised his hand to retaliate, and she shoved it hard against the top of the couch. She grabbed his other arm as well, twisting and pinning it. She straddled him, using her pent-up desire to fuel her strength. She knocked the knife from his hand.

"I'll tell you what I'll give you," she said.

"Yeah?" he grunted, thrusting his hips against her.

"I'm going to give you my timidity." She kissed him hard. "And I'm going to give you my shame." She kissed him again, starting to grind against him. "And in return, you are going to give me whatever I want."

"My pleasure," he said, twisting his arms free.

They fought, struggling to gain the upper hand. Had he been himself, she likely would have lost. But Peter's body was not muscular. Still, it was a hard fight.

He tore her blouse with a sharp pull when she bit the curve of his neck. She ripped the pants from him, freeing his cock. She laughed as the dragon's head was revealed, threatening to chew off his balls. "Like teeth, do you?"

"I like pain, lovie," he sniggered, digging his fingernails into the small of her back. He pulled her against him roughly, nails biting into her flesh.

She grabbed his hair, pulled his head back sharply and slapped him when he shouted.

"You'll wake the neighbors, dear," she grunted, thrusting against him. She jammed her lips against his, sucking and biting, and felt him bruising hers in return. His fingers tangled in her hair, pain like fire in her scalp.

He squeezed her tits, his teeth catching her nipples. She moaned, intensely aware of the heat between her legs. He tried to pull away her panties, but she grabbed his hand and shoved it away. She scrabbled for the knife as they slammed their bodies together.

They shoved and pressed and ground their way through the apartment to the bedroom, fighting to keep dominance. He threw her prone over the edge the bed, mounting her from behind.

"Fucking bitch," he grunted, sliding his cock against her through her soaking panties.

She crawled farther up the bed as he tore her skirt and pantyhose away. She rolled over as he climbed onto her, her chest heaving, leaning back to allow him access. He grinned victoriously and forced down her panties.

When they were off, she kicked him in the stomach.

He toppled onto her, and she wrapped her legs around him to flip them both over.

"I thought we understood each other," she whispered almost pleasantly. "I paid you. I decide how this goes." She squeezed his cock, her nails scraping into him. He shrieked. She covered his mouth, her hand pressing the knife against his chin. "Nod."

He did.

She lowered herself onto him, bucking hard. She had been wanting this all night—every night, for a thousand nights.

She could feel the sun coming up behind her, the warm rays licking her skin, her sweat burning in the scrapes on her back. She imagined it like a third lover in the room, goading her on as she pounded against the man pinned beneath her. He gasped and groaned, and she fucked him harder with every sound, bending to lick the sweat from his chest and bite his pebble-like nipples, savagely delighting in the taste of his body.

When she looked up again, Peter was looking back at her.

Her orgasm tore through her roughly, and she crashed against him, her clit pulsing against the base of his shaft. She was dimly aware of Peter's cum pumping into her, his own yelps intertwining with her cries.

They stared at each other as they caught their breath.

"Morning, Pete," she said finally. She ran her fingers softly over his bicep, where the dragon had been moments before.

"Annette?" he said. "What was that?"

"Fun," she said. She was exhausted. She fell asleep against him, the sheets twined around them.

She woke up in her office on campus, papers sticking to her cheek.

She sat up as though struck by lightning. What the hell had happened?

She looked at the clock. 11:08 p.m. Had she fallen asleep while marking papers?

Her head ached. The carnival, the fucking—

"I am overworked," she announced to her empty office. "I am going crazy."

She examined the pile of essays still on her desk. She decided to take them home.

As she picked them up, a few cards fluttered out from between the pages.

She started. Some, she recognized. Herself, hanging upside down. A devil in a purple waistcoat and a velvet hat.

Some were blank. And some were new.

THE TOWER, one announced, a Ferris wheel coming loose from its moorings. TWENTY was her, standing triumphant over a serpent.

THE SUN, her own face, beatific, mouth open in ecstasy, haloed in gold.

XXI was Peter and her entwined, naked and scarred, the sheet wrapped around them as they floated in space.

A note was taped to the back of this last one.

My dear, I will always regret our lost opportunity, but I think it had the intended effect in the end. Congratulations! But the journey is never over— the cycle just begins again. Do come back, if ever you are stuck. My hirsute darling June and I would love to have you, in as many ways as we can. Bring your chap if you'd like. It was signed with a pictograph of a top hat.

She went home.

Peter stirred when she came to bed. "Annie," he said sleepily. "I had the strangest dream."

"Oh?"

"You were like a—Valkyrie, descending from heaven for me." He shifted, and she could see his erection beneath the thin sheet.

"Did you like it?" she asked, leaning over him. Her hair trailed over him, brushing against his chest softly.

He shuddered. "Yes," he said shyly. "I think so."

"Good," she said and climbed onto him. She wouldn't need to go back.

Waking

A.D.R. Forte

She had come because of Pig, and Pig had deserted her tonight, pleading a sore throat and achy feet. She ought to go home too, she thought, instead of staying and shouting herself hoarse across a table sticky with spilled drinks, at people she didn't particularly like, who were too drunk to care what she said anyway.

She stayed because her eyes kept going back to the dance floor and the bodies twirling there, flashing in and out of reality, illuminated by stark light, then swallowed by dark again, then light again.

Easier too to stay put and slowly drink until she'd gotten sufficiently numb not to feel the cold while she waited for a cab. Go home then and fall into bed and dreamless sleep.

It had been a very, very long time since she'd dreamed. That was probably for the best. Before, the dreams had always meant trouble, but she was past that now.

That had been long, long ago.

* * *

In the club's restroom she stood under the harsh glare of the fluorescent light over the mirror and wiped smudged mascara. She'd worn too much and the bright restroom didn't offer any kindan of reprieve. Grimacing, she crumpled and dropped one blackened square of Kleenex on the metal counter and reached for another square. She didn't look around when the door opened and a male figure appeared in her peripheral vision.

Unisex restrooms in places such as this didn't shock her. It was one of a great many other things that should have been unacceptable to her daylight self. The self that wore dark, tailored suits and drove an unassuming and very expensive car.

A shadow self.

"My God. Alice?"

She jabbed herself in the eye, startled by that voice: a voice that didn't belong here, a voice that had to be impossible. She turned, blinking, hoping she'd been wrong. But no.

He stood there, hands in pockets, with his usual superior smirk. As if he knew something the rest of the world didn't. He might have just stepped out of the daylight world except for the clothes: the black silk shirt, the brocade waistcoat and the sparkle of silver at his neck.

Finn Leverett didn't wear clothes like that, and Finn Leverett had no business being here.

She dabbed at her watering eye, conscious that mascara and eyeliner were trailing new black lines

178

down her cheek. But why should a little smeared makeup matter? Could it take away the rest of her current attire and transform her back into the pastel shadow self? Take them out of here and transplant them somewhere more acceptable?

Anger heated her face and chest. Why did he have to invade this tiny part of her life that she kept free of the façade? Pollute it by making her remember who she was. He belonged to that world. Upstairs. Clean shirts and garden parties.

"AJ," she said, correcting his infuriating use of her name, just as she always had. Just as he'd always insisted on calling her Alice. His smirk deepened. "I thought you moved," she said, ignoring it. "Something about needing a continent between you and my stepmother?"

He laughed at that and ran a hand through his hair.

"I did say that. Didn't I?" His hand went back into his pocket and he shrugged. He glanced to the side, at her reflection caught in the mirror. "Another thing I was wrong about, I guess. But you know, even indignation burns itself out after a while." He looked back at her and the smirk returned. "But then, you've never been indignant a day in your life, have you, Alice? You don't care about anything enough to get angry."

The restroom door banged open again, saving her a response as a girl in a scarlet corset laughed shrilly. When the drunken patrons had shuffled past them, she looked at him and shrugged in imitation of his own gesture before.

"Nice to see you again, Finn. You're as charming as ever."

"Likewise."

He started to walk past her and she took a breath, glad this uncomfortable, impossible encounter was over. Then she froze. He stood right beside her, so close their hips almost touched. She tilted her head back to meet his gaze, defying shame, and he smiled.

"You look nice." His fingers brushed the ruffled lace edge of her sleeve. "This suits you."

For a heartbeat she stared at him, speechless, trying to find the touch of sarcasm, the hidden insult in the words, but she failed. He couldn't mean it. He had to be laughing at her, but she couldn't see it.

It made her feel like she'd lost her balance. Was falling. Again.

No. No, that was just the alcohol and the end of a long day. When she'd first seen Finn Leverett, her stepmother's new chairman and latest lover, she'd felt the same. Like the ground had slid out from under her, inexplicably and very fast, and there was something she ought to remember. Something important.

But then, like now, it had been an illusion.

He was attractive. He was young, younger perhaps than she herself. He was flirtatious, brilliant and rather shameless, and that explained the confusion and the reason her heart beat too fast.

Now, like then, she had to put it out of mind and not just because of their awkward social connection.

Finn's effect on her made her a bit giddy, made her feel a bit unreal and not quite herself. He was too many Jell-O shots on an empty stomach. He was creepy movies in the middle of the night with not enough sleep.

Feeling this way was dangerous. Unhealthy. She imagined a doctor in a white coat, frowning at the floating sensation in her head.

She forced her painted lips into a smile and arched one nonchalant eyebrow.

"What a nice thing to say," she managed. "Thank you."

Then she made her legs move, made them carry her to the door with steps that seemed ungainly and unsteady and much too slow. She didn't look back at him.

* * *

Darkness and noise enveloped her like a giant blanket. She closed her eyes for an instant and leaned against the wall to catch her breath. Just a few minutes of time, yet she was drained as if she'd been running for hours.

She pushed away and someone stumbled into her. A pretty boy with spiky hair, a spiked collar and lips as brightly painted as hers. He steadied them both and smiled at her, put an encouraging hand on her hip, but she pushed him away. No. She had to leave. Now.

Ignore the siren call of the dance floor, now and for the foreseeable future. She couldn't risk running into *him* again, not here. If he was back in town, she'd see him enough in the daylight world, and that would be bad enough. Would have been bad enough without tonight.

She pushed her way through warm bodies. Her hands touched bare arms cool with sweat from the dance floor. She smelled perfume and sweat and alcohol.

Here she felt almost real. Almost alive.

She didn't want to spend week after week making up excuses to Pig and the other few she called friends for why she couldn't join them until they finally gave up and left her to drink herself oblivious, alone in her spotless uptown apartment.

Damn Finn. It only added salt to the wound that he so fit the picture of what she wanted, with his dark hair and elegant face. *Bad thinking.* Why did her mind insist on chasing after absurd, unacceptable things?

At least she'd made it through the crowd now and halfway up the stairs that would take her to the entrance. Ahead of her: silence and cold. Behind her, the dance floor thrummed and moved, hot and sensual and dark.

A hand closed over her elbow, startling her. But even as she turned, she knew.

* * *

She could smell his scent, feel the heat of his body behind hers, his breath on her neck as he leaned close enough to be heard.

"You can't be leaving."

She nodded, started to say something about having to go. He couldn't have heard her, but it didn't matter. He shook his head, cutting her off, and slid his hand down her arm to her wrist. He led her the rest of the way up the stairs to where the noise receded and pulled her to the side, into the shelter of a draped curtain. It muted the music enough for them to talk, cut them off from prying eyes.

Folds of red velvet hung behind him, and his shirt collar had pulled apart enough to reveal the links of the silver chain. It rested just at the hollow above his collarbones, and she tried her best not to stare at it. She tried her best not to stare at all but knew she failed miserably. His eyes, vibrant blue even in the dim light, didn't help either.

"You aren't leaving because of me, are you?"

There wasn't any escape this time. She took a breath and shook her head, but not to deny his words.

"You have to admit. This is awkward."

He lifted an eyebrow. "Why? I've seen... your stepmother. We were civil."

"I didn't mean that. I mean... Well no. That's just it, isn't it?"

Her gaze, flickering from place to place in a futile effort to find a safe landing place, found his mouth. Judgment slowed by alcohol and tiredness, she didn't look away. Not fast enough.

He reached out and she felt his fingers dragging one curl of her hair downward. She closed her eyes, felt the whisper of his skin, the backs of his fingers against her bare shoulder before he released the curl. She felt the hair brush her neck as it bounced free.

She opened her eyes.

"Come on." He gestured with his head in the direction of the dance floor, reached to take her hand.

She pulled back, putting her hand behind her even

though she realized, too late, that the posture looked both childlike and seductive. Face burning, she shook her head.

"I can't."

He waited, looking at her with sarcastic, beautiful eyes.

"Can't dance with me?"

"No." She looked at the edge of his shoulder, at a tiny bit of black silk cloth. A safe thing to look at. She refused to turn to him, even though she could feel his gaze on her face. Knew he saw her burning with longing and with shame.

"Is it really any sense of propriety? Or is it just pride?"

Goaded past endurance, she had to look at him. Bastard. But how could she explain it was neither? That she couldn't even explain it to herself.

He put her all out of proportion.

"Maybe it's a bit of both. Oh hell, I don't know," she said miserably.

He laughed and shook his head.

"I should have known I'd get an honest answer."

For a heartbeat he contemplated her, then he turned and lifted the edge of the curtain. Music, loud, the rhythmic pulse of a great beast, swept toward them. He looked back at her.

"The invitation stands, my dear." A pause. "If it makes a difference, I never slept with her. We just let everyone think so."

Sensible. Provide enough salacious gossip that no one looked too closely into what the boardroom discussed. Part of why the Red Heart Group had stunned the market with not one, but two acquisitions under Finn's genius. Until even he had had enough of her stepmother's tempers and impossible demands.

She believed him. There wasn't any question about it.

In one smooth motion, he stepped beyond the barrier of the curtain and waited, looking at her. She stared back, heart pounding in her throat. He put one hand across his chest and gave her the ghost of a bow. Light glittered on the silver of his chain. Then between one blink and another, he'd walked back into the darkness.

As fast as her shoes would allow, she followed.

* * *

She glimpsed him disappearing into the crowd at the foot of the stairs. "Oh wait," she whispered. A sound so insignificant it might not have existed at all, but by the time she made it down the stairs, she'd lost sight of him entirely. Where the press thinned near the walls, she paused, straining to make sense of writhing shapes in the spinning light, aware of the futility of her efforts.

Stupid to think she could find him again that easily. She might spend the entire night searching and not run into him again. He might leave after all.

Biting her lip, she backed up to where the wall provided solid reassurance. The wall was real even if nothing else was. She hadn't eaten enough. Hadn't slept enough. Had a bit too much to drink. And then Finn.

She had stepped into the dreams again. Wide awake this time. But there were no frowning doctors now. No sensible voices. No medication.

This time her stepmother would not be understanding, and this time she was alone. Pig and the others belonged to the dependable world in their own way. They couldn't reach her here.

Fear burned at the back of her throat. Trembling, she opened her eyes.

To dark. Stillness.

* * *

A room with hidden corners, walls stretching away into shadow, giving the appearance they didn't end at all. From no discernible source, a faint bloom of light showed her the floor, the smooth black tiles cut into squares by thin, green lines. Her shoes clicked on the surface as she took a handful of halting steps forward. Without looking around she knew there would be no concrete and plaster nightclub wall behind her, just the room stretching away in the other direction.

She'd been here before. Long ago.

Somewhere in the half-darkness ahead, a door slammed. Holding her breath, she listened. Only silence and the nervous sound of her own breath.

Nothing to be afraid of, she told herself. Just one foot in front of the other and sooner or later she'd find a door. There were always doors.

Yes, there's one now.

Polished wood and a golden doorknob shining in

the light. Light that grew stronger as she drew closer even while the rest of the hallway slipped into shadow behind her. She reached for the knob, heart knocking hard enough against her ribs that she suspected it might very well fly out of her mouth and fall on the floor.

That proved she still had a heart at least, and it had known when she followed Finn where she would end up. Maybe it had led her back here.

"It's my name after all," she said aloud. In this quiet, her voice sounded louder and stronger than it usually did. Heiress to the Red Heart. Strange how she never thought of herself that way.

Under her hand, the knob turned with a click and the light dimmed. *The light follows me*, she thought. But she wouldn't need it outside. She opened the door and went into the garden beyond.

* * *

Starlight, much brighter than starlight should be, lit the white stones of the path, and a deep breath brought her the scent of the roses, faint on the chilly air. In another week or two the last of the blooms would fall and the frost would follow. But for now she had them.

Shivering a little, rubbing her arms, she turned down the path. He was waiting for her.

"I see you decided to take my invitation."

His voice held laughter, but gentle this time. Conversational. He touched her again. A hand on her arm brought her to a halt before him, and starlight showed her the lines of his mouth, the skin taut over one arched cheekbone now shadowed by the hint of stubble. Was it five-o'clock shadow? Or 2:00 a.m. shadow?

She wasn't sure how time even existed here, or if it followed the rules. She wasn't following the rules, if there were any.

Smiling, he reached into a waistcoat pocket and drew out something that flashed silver in his hand.

"Close enough. Two twenty-seven," he said.

She laughed, and he slipped the watch back, looked at her.

"Shouldn't you be in bed?"

She drew her fingers down that cheek and watched the shift of his jaw at the contact. Rough friction against the skin on the backs of her fingers tingled through her body. Curious and sweet. Beneath her corseted bodice and blouse, she felt her nipples becoming aware of his body, aware of his lust.

His lips were chapped just a little, bruised from the same bad habit she had of biting them out of nerves or impatience, but the curve of their shape promised shameless kisses. She pulled his head down to hers and let her tongue flicker across his lower lip, tasting him. He breathed in, short and sharp, and she sensed every muscle in him tensing. His hands had closed warm on her waist, and her shivering now had nothing to do with cold.

She had remembered, and her head was clearer than it had been in a long, long time. Finn wasn't innocent, if he ever had been. And neither was she, anymore.

"No," she told him. "I don't have to be."

* * *

He took her hand and they broke into a run. She had a thought that the patent-leather shoes with the chunky soles were not made for running, but she ran all the same. He led her around a turn in the path, passed beneath an archway in the tall hedges flanking the path. The breath burned in her chest and her throat, and she wondered if she had enough to shout at him and ask him to stop. But before that there was another arch, a wall beyond that, tangled with ivy and climbing roses. He pulled her into the recess between stone and hedge, and she leaned against the stone, fighting for breath.

He stole it from her with his mouth on hers, his tongue finding the shape of her lips before sliding between them while his hands moved up her thighs, lifting and crumpling her skirt. Their clothes still held the scent of sweat and smoke and spilled drinks. Her feet ached in the impossible shoes.

But it didn't matter. His touch on her body was no careful romance. Just lust, awake and dangerous.

Like here.

He undid the laces of her bodice, and the loose sleeves of her blouse slipped nearly to her elbows. He pushed them farther down, off her hands and down around her hips. Lace and cotton and mesh fell in a heap at her feet, and she kicked it away. He was studying her silently: bare from the waist up, nipples tight with need, lips swollen from kisses, hair and mascara in a state she couldn't even begin to imagine. She saw his throat move as he swallowed.

189

She had entirely forgotten what being herself felt like, and yet every touch of air, every whisper of his breath or caress of fingers on her skin made perfect sense. She was real. She was alive.

She licked her lips and lifted her bare arms to him.

"Fuck me," she said.

* * *

"In a moment," he replied. He moved to kneel at her feet, and she felt his hands on her bare ass, raising her hips, throwing her off-balance. Again. But balance wasn't important here.

He didn't offer her soft kisses or teasing promises of delight. That wasn't what she wanted. Instead his hands held her thighs wide and her skirt bunched while he flicked his tongue hard over her clit. She gasped at the surge of need, her teeth automatically finding her lower lip to savage it as he rocked her against his mouth. Pain warred with need.

She didn't know if she writhed against his bruising teeth and sucking mouth out of a desire for escape or because she craved more of the exquisite arousal. Maybe both. But it was too hard to think about that with the pounding blood in her head and the need in her cunt. Too hard to think at all.

But better this than numb. Never again. Not ever again.

Finn was murmuring words that had no shape and no sense against her wetness. It maddened her, the sweet hum of his voice on her like that. When he let go of her ass with one hand and slipped a finger inside her, she barely managed to turn the scream that wanted to burst free into a moan.

He slid a second finger in, then a third for an instant before he twisted his hand and she felt the pressure of his touch at her ass. She was so wet and she'd made such an utter mess of his fingers that he invaded her ass with almost-ease. Not that she would have cared. She'd forgotten what reasonable felt like too.

She only needed to come.

"Yes," he said, low and rough, gazing up at her as his fingers moved in her cunt and her ass and rubbed her sore clit. "Come for me."

She shook her head, but the first ripple of orgasm was already flowing through her muscles. Her mouth was dry and her head spinning. She could see his eyes, blue gaze bright and intent with a need that matched her own as he punished and pleasured her.

The light follows me, she thought. Then she was falling again, far and fast, and on and on and on.

* * *

"My sweet little tart."

His voice at her shoulder made her open her eyes. He stood over her, hands to either side to support her weight. She felt the bulge of his crotch pressing against her, and though her body still shuddered with the weakness of climax, her lust hadn't been stilled. Not yet.

"I've hungered for you," he said.

"Steal me, then," she answered. "And I promise you won't be punished too much."

Had she said that? Yes, she had. She saw it in his eyes. He deferred to her now. Served at her behest, even as he spun her to face the wall and positioned her hands on the stones.

Thorny leaves from the vines pricked at her fingers, sharp, sudden counterpoint to the slow ache between her legs. A hungry ache that only intensified as she felt the thick head of his cock pressing the lips of her cunt. His fingers had bruised her. His cock stretched her, growing bigger with each thrust, it seemed. Larger and larger. She could feel each knotted, ridged vein rubbing the sensitive walls of her cunt as he thrust. And each time the tip of that wondrous cock met her flesh with all the force of his body behind it, she could have died. Quite easily.

But she didn't have any plans to die just yet. Not until she'd come again, at least. She whimpered, and with a breathless laugh he asked if that if that was big enough to satisfy her. She couldn't answer, grinding herself against him. Pleased with the satisfying slap every time her ass met his hips, the rustle of her skirt crushed between them, with the grunt from him as she grew wetter and wetter. Tighter and tighter.

His hands found her naked breasts and her nipples, barely cupping them. Just enough to send sensation flooding to her clit as his fingers brushed them. Not enough to stop the delicious, swaying heaviness as their bodies moved apart and slammed together again.

Queen and knave.

Oh, I can't bear any more, she thought. The stones were slipping under her sweating fingers, or maybe it was the wall itself falling away instead. Ivy and roses and wall and hedge all tumbling away from her and Finn. But they were a steady, demanding frenzy dancing on the edge of pain. They were rising, faster. Gasp and grunt and strain a little more, a little bit more, before she floated off entirely.

He moaned her name, and she felt his body shudder hard. She was melting. Spilling over.

They were both falling, down and down and down.

* * *

And into the tangle of sheets. Her bed. Even in the dark she recognized the familiar shapes of her room, the laundry scent of her pillows and blankets.

The damned shoes were still on and still killing her feet. She kicked them off and heard Finn shift behind her. He sat up, and brushed back the strands of her loosened hair so he could see her face.

"Darling, Alice."

She didn't bother to correct him.

Through the lace of curtains she could see the outline of blue. The daylight world was waking up, but she didn't have to fall asleep to exist in it. Didn't have to fear dreams—or herself—ever again.

"It's time for breakfast, dear," Finn said.

She turned to him and ran her hand along his definitely rough cheek. His shirt and waistcoat hung loose, buttons askew and plainly showing the silver chain, the dust of dark hair against the pale skin of his chest. Blue eyes caught the meager light. He was quite beautiful.

"My Queen," he whispered.

"I'm still dreaming," she said.

He answered her with a kiss.

The Boiling Sea
Angela Caperton

I met the Walrus in July 1969, my first full day back in the world. Sometimes I think everything that happened after that was only a dream, all the decades just fantasy or hallucination, but I know better. Everything changed, but it's all as real as flying pigs, as certain as cabbages.

I came back from Nam that summer and, after my discharge, I went home for a bad afternoon and evening, just long enough for my parents to remind me why I'd enlisted the very moment I turned eighteen. Around 4:00 a.m., jacked up on white cross and thermos coffee, I took my old Ford and headed for the nearest coast, through lowland fog, to a crackling soundtrack of Top Forty radio and clear channel preachers. I wanted a taste of what I'd been reading about in magazines back in country: hippie girls, California pot and loud, beautiful music. I had nearly three thousand dollars and no ambition but to have a dangerously good time.

Not long after sunrise, I rolled up in a little resort town called Waling. You probably know a place just like it. Two thousand souls in the winter and ten thousand in the summer. The citizens complain about the tourists while they sell cases of beer and suntan oil. I parked the Galaxy in a dusty lot, near a hippie bus painted in psychedelic colors, and walked down to the waterfront.

Speed and sleeplessness broke golden sunlight into jagged pieces on the ocean. A boardwalk ran several hundred feet along the shore, and I saw a café at the end of it. I walked in that direction, first on the sand and then the boardwalk. Both seemed like clouds beneath my feet. I was a free man. No one was trying to kill me. I was exhausted and frayed, but deliriously happy to be alive.

A few early shop workers watched me pass, probably making me as a tourist or trouble or both. None of the shops were open yet and I didn't pay much attention to them, but I stopped outside the big stucco building beside the café. The peeling marquee read *Theatre de Fantasia*, and a banner painted in Day-Glo heralded a show called *Alice, Baby!* Below it, I saw a sign: *Help Wanted. Maintenance and set construction. See Julian.*

I headed on to the café, a place called Red's. Most of the booths were full, and I saw a lot of young, friendly faces, some of them female and beautiful.

I thought Waling might not be so bad a place to spend some time, so I took one of the last seats at the counter and ordered toast and coffee from a pretty, middle-aged woman who called me "hon." Even buttered bread sounded like too much food, but the ache in my gut said I needed to eat. The waitress must've seen the crazy look in my eyes, because she hovered over me and smiled when I'd finished. The food anchored me enough to smile back at her. Her name tag said *Velma.*

"Saw the sign next door," I told Velma. "You know Julian?"

"Oh, hon, everybody knows Julian. He'll be along any minute." She sized me up. "You going to work for him?"

I looked around the diner. Everyone else had resumed breakfast and morning chatter. "Maybe. It's a theater? He shows movies?"

"Other kind of theater. Julian writes plays, and his actors perform them on summer weekends. The tourists love them. The kids, you know?"

"He owns the theater and writes the plays? Is he rich?"

"Must be," Velma said, taking my plate and refilling my coffee. "Anyway, you'll like it here. Lots of folks your age this summer. Hippies." She said the word with amusement and no animosity at all. "Some of them live in town, and lots more stay at the Marlin, on East 38. Some of the kids call it a commune, but it's just an old motor court. You need a place to stay, maybe they can help you out. I'd rent you a room, but Ronnie'd kill me." She winked at me and sauntered off to wait on an old man at the other end of the counter.

I watched her walk away, and when I turned back around, the Walrus sat on the stool beside me. Dark hair pulled back in a tail, he looked like that guy in the Byrds, David Crosby, but bigger and heavier. He was older than me too, maybe ten years older, and he had the biggest, darkest eyes of anyone I ever knew.

"I'm Julian Brightstar," he said. "What's your name?"

"Tom," I told him. "Tom Rimer."

"You know which end of a hammer to hold on to?"

"I do, for a fact. Army construction and summer jobs before that."

"Ten bucks a day and a place to sleep." Julian grinned at me. "No hassles at all, man. You in?"

"Sure. When do I start?"

"Right now. I need a set built by Friday night. And you need to meet the players. You ever do any acting?"

I shook my head, but when I followed Julian out of Red's Café, I felt the gaze of every eye in the place, like I was already on his stage. As we stepped onto the boardwalk, I saw a bearded man the color of ashes skulking in the little alley between Red's and the theater, a beach bum in the last stages of bumming before he becomes a corpse or a guest of the county. Half in shadow, he watched us pass with shattered eyes, and I wondered what hell had given him such a stare.

The Theatre de Fantasia smelled like incense and mildew, but I caught the sweet scent of weed in the mix, so I wasn't surprised when Julian offered me a twisted, yellow joint. He locked the door behind us as I lit up, drawing the spicy smoke deep in my chest. I'd smoked a few times in Nam, but over there, even in Saigon, it made me so paranoid I couldn't stop my hands from shaking. Home on leave, when I blew a number with the guys, I was fine. Julian's pot tasted strong, and my head turned nicely into muted Day-Glo mush by the third hit.

Julian led me through the little lobby and into the theater. Built for movies back when movie theaters still had stages, the place might have held two hundred people, except most of the seats in back had been pulled out by the roots. The only light in the cavernous space came from backstage, flickering orange, red and yellow, like a fire.

The pot spun my head, and each step took me farther and farther from all the things I wanted to leave behind. We walked carefully up the steps to the stage and then back into the wings. The light came from a big room behind the screen, lit by a lamp hung with a slowly rotating shade that scattered flame colors across the walls and ceiling. Almost a dozen kids, boys and girls, sat around a little table or sprawled on mattresses. Flats and decorated set pieces lined one wall. A vivid ocean and a painted beach stretched into a false forever.

As my eyes adjusted to the whirling light, I saw that some of the girls in the room were naked, maybe some of the guys too, but my gaze glued to a redhead stretched out on one of the mattresses. She lay there, bare and open, like the most natural thing in the world, and I saw the whirling fire in her eyes, the long, straight mane of her hair and the tangled flame of her bush.

My cock grew three sizes in my jeans, and Julian laughed. "Welcome to Wonderland, Tom," he said, and everyone laughed, joyous and inviting. Someone clapped me on the back, and I looked around to see a tall, dark kid, maybe nineteen, shirtless and muscled like a lifeguard. He offered me another joint, and I blew away the last shreds of my sanity.

I remember laughter and dancing, everyone crazy happy. Two of the chicks stayed naked, and we took turns, blindfolded, exploring them with our hands, trying to guess who was who. I learned their names. Sheena, the redhead, and Cowgirl, a brunette with wide hips, nice tits and a wild giggle.

Then the girls had their turn.

"Get naked, Tom," Julian told me and I remember thinking, *What the hell.* This was everything I wanted. "Lorina, Sheena, Beth, Cowgirl, make him feel welcome."

Two of them held me down with tender force: Lorina, a beautiful blonde, the youngest girl in the room, surely no more than eighteen, wearing a long, blue, simple cotton dress; and Beth, a black girl who smiled but never laughed, dressed in a t-shirt and short shorts. They gripped my bare arms and held me while Sheena and Cowgirl worked me over with their hands, not quite touching my aching cock, but massaging every muscle in my arms and legs, my back and my hips, their touch soft as feathers but firm as coarse leather. Everything fell away from me, the blaring, bloody days in Nam, the rough ride home, home itself, until I lay in a pleasurable coma of lust.

"Okay, Sheena," Julian commanded, "blow him."

All that remained of my tension was in the seven plus inches of heat she took between her lips. She cupped my balls, pulled me deeper than the girls in Saigon, fearless. She worked for only a moment, slow but insistent, and I came in an endless explosion of fevered dream, the rushing road before my car, the passage out of darkness and into the dawn, into the here and now.

Into Wonderland.

* * *

After a while, people drifted away, and I slept a little on a mat in that dark room. Sheena, dressed now in jeans and a stomach-baring fringed top, woke me with a kiss.

"Get dressed. We're going to have rehearsals on the beach." She ran her hands over my shoulders and hips, finally catching my hardening cock in her hand and caressing the head. "Cannot wait for you to fuck me," she purred. "But Julian wants us now." She released me, and I pulled my jeans on, my thoughts a tumble of fog and lust. "No shirt, baby," she said and licked my right nipple. "So I can touch you."

We traipsed out of the theater and down the boardwalk to the bus I had seen in the lot when I drove in. The front of it had been painted with the face of a white rabbit, the hazy headlights its eyes, front bumper flocked with stiff, wiry whiskers, long cartoon ears airbrushed all down both sides of the vehicle. Beautifully painted flowers scattered before the rabbit's charge, every petal detailed and beautiful.

Under a scrubby tree, at the edge of the parking lot, I saw the ash-faced bum I had seen in the morning. He watched as we boarded the bus. No one paid any attention to him, but I felt a stab of empathy. I now recognized the look in his eyes. I knew it from men in country, men who had seen bad things, or who had done worse things. I wondered who he was.

Aboard the bus, I wanted to sit with Sheena, but Julian had saved a spot for me in the seat just behind the driver, an enormous Nordic kid named Lars.

"Everyone is in the play," Julian said, not looking at me, but staring out the window as the bus maneuvered out of the parking lot full of families, kids running seemingly everywhere, bright, summer chaos. "I'll give you a role too," he said. "Maybe more than one."

"It's a play for kids?" I asked. Out of the lot, the bus bumped down State Sixty, past trailer camps and motel crossroads, everything sun-bleached and holy to my shattered eyes. "Called *Alice, Baby*?"

"For the kiddies, yeah," Julian said and laughed. "But the mamas and papas have to dig it too. You ever read Alice?"

"Like in Wonderland? No." I knew the book was regarded as cool, even trippy, but I didn't read many books. I'd heard the Jefferson Airplane song.

"I saw the movie," I said. "And one pill makes you smaller."

"That movie was a mindfuck," Julian said. "All that heavy shit right there in the heads of a whole generation, man. Even Walt Disney couldn't fuck that up."

I had no idea what he meant, but I nodded and focused past Julian on the seats across the aisle, where Sheena and Lorina sat, the baby blonde on the aisle. I stared—I couldn't help it. She was pale as white porcelain; the afternoon light through the bus windows was warm on everyone else, but she looked like snow, her hair fair as sun on glass, too bright to look directly at.

Julian followed my gaze and grinned.

"She's our Alice," he said. "Every tale of Wonderland has to have an Alice, the wise innocent who falls into strange days, brother. Alice is like America, dig?"

Once again, I had no idea what he meant, but I nodded and said, "I dig."

We rode in the rabbit bus a couple of miles down the coast, by bait stands and bars, then we took a narrow turnoff to a desolate stretch of beach, a shore of gray sand sloping down to choppy surf, too rough for swimming or surfing. The sunlight capered on whitecaps and kissed my bare shoulders with well-being as I helped unload the bus, blankets and a crate of food and drink.

They rehearsed with the sea as a backdrop, a lot of giggling at first, but then the players fell into their work, and I listened and watched awhile. Mostly Julian made them dance, repeating the steps of a complicated reel, critical but funny as he corrected the steps and timing.

"If you can dance on the sand," he told them three or four times, "you can dance anywhere. Today you are nothing but a pack of cards. Shuffle and deal, brothers and sisters."

I watched, hypnotized. Cards, of course. I saw it the way Julian wanted it to be, the dancers' choreographed movements suggesting dovetails and overhand shuffling, mixing and separating again. "When they wear the costumes, the effect will be perfect," Julian said with a triumphant smile.

They were certainly not wearing costumes now. Most of the kids had initially worn t-shirts and bathing suits, but the shirts had all come off and they all danced nearly naked on the shore of the sea, all except Alice—Lorina—who wore her thin, blue dress, translucent when she danced against the slanting sun.

At the end of the rehearsal, Alice danced alone at the center of the pack, the whirling treys and tens not quite approaching her, but others, Sheena and Lars, grew bolder, and began to pull at her arms, spinning her among the cavorting deck. The dance became a riot of flailing arms and kicking legs, sand like powdered diamonds in the merciless sun, and the pack of cards fell, almost naked, glistening with sweat, onto Alice, all of them laughing like children.

* * *

We ate rice, drank tea, smoked hash and watched the sun burn in a slow crawl down the sky to the juncture of sea and sand. Waling was barely visible around the curving coast. Sheena sat close, leaning on me, her bare breasts a constant heat against my arm or my chest, her hand always on my thigh or my back, fingers firm and warm as brands.

Everyone seemed lost in a mellow fog, and Sheena's voice startled me when she asked, "Did you know Julian is a magician?"

"Stupid," I grunted. "Magic is lies and tricks."

The collective, stoned consciousness of the group focused on my words. They laughed at me. My breathing quickened, and I pushed back a surge of anger.

Julian eased himself out of Beth's arms, stood up and loomed over me, his shape dark against the red sky.

"No," Julian said. "It's not." His tone was light, gently mocking. "We're all magicians, Tom. We turn food to shit and time into garbage, wasting our lives with trivia when the real world is only waiting for us to see it."

"Real world?" I growled. Sheena scooted back as I staggered to my feet. "You don't know what 'real' is!" I tried to punch the air to make my point, but my arms remained immobile at my sides, too heavy to support my message.

"You think you know what is real?" Julian asked, grinning. "The only reality, Thomas, is the one we make of dreams and numbers. Lewis Carroll—Charles Dodgson—had genius for both. He knew how to open the door behind the laughing knob, and I, I am learning how too."

"That's a load of crap," I spat. The whole troupe held its breath. I imagined them falling on me, swords and spades, cutting me to pieces. But Julian only watched with a smile until his smile was all I could see.

"Where are you going?" he asked.

"Nowhere," I answered. "Everywhere."

"Then it doesn't really matter which way you go, does it? Walk with us awhile. *You can leave whenever you want to.*"

"Tom," Sheena said, and I turned to where she half

reclined on the sand. She had shucked her shorts so she lay entirely nude beneath the stars and moon, the dark red-golden bush between her legs a shadow that concealed amazing things. I forgot my anger, forgot Julian's bullshit. In the dark, Sheena's eyes glowed and her lips shone like blood petals. I dropped to my knees, hardly daring to reach out and touch her, but needing to fuck her just as much as I needed to breathe.

Her eyes, her lips, the dark-tipped moons of her breasts, her hands reaching out to pull my shorts down... I saw each of her charms in isolation: total, divine. I forgot everyone in the troupe, everyone in the world, except the girl who stretched out beneath me. As I moved onto her, Sheena faded away unless I looked directly at her, her eyes suspended in the darkness, her lips, her tongue... then I was in her, our bodies gritty with sand, hot enough to become glass, fused like my cock in her pussy, grinding, and I neither knew nor wanted anything in the world but her cunt, her core, and I would do anything to have her.

In that moment, I knew only Sheena's sweet pussy, but later, when I thought of the beach, I remembered Julian watching us.

Grinning like a cat.

* * *

I woke with sand between my teeth and mud in my brain, sprawled on one of the mattresses in the back of the Theatre de Fantasia, naked, with Sheena wrapped around me, sticky and hot. She rubbed against my thigh, and I woke up a little and then she rolled to straddle me and ground her crotch against mine. I was only half-hard when she caught my cock and tucked it into her pussy, but the motion of her hips brought me to erection and she rode me in slow waves, her fingernails sharp in my shoulders, her eyes wide and hungry. We came together in a slow, rolling rush of sensation, and she settled atop me, her hips still working just a little, milking me.

Some of the others in the troupe were already awake, and pretty soon we got up and dressed too. Julian led us down to Red's, and we filled three booths with spillover. Julian insisted I sit with him at the bar.

Velma smiled at me and winked. "Found a job, eh?" I wanted to talk to her, but Julian caught me by the shoulder and turned me to face him.

"Serious question, Tom," he said. "Who are you?"

My head hurt, but Sheena had left me with a sweet edge even Julian couldn't temper.

"I'm a free man," I told him.

"That's not what I mean," he laughed, his moustache twitching and his jowls shaking. His eyes sparkled kindly, but very dark. "Who will you be in the play? You must have a role."

"I don't know. Can't I just be a carpenter?"

"Oh my word," he said and laughed. "It is so obvious I didn't see it. You shall be. You will be the Carpenter."

We ate our breakfasts and Julian paid for them. I left a two dollar tip for Velma and winked at her. She didn't wink back. I saw something in her eyes that might have been worry, and I told myself I'd come back and talk to her soon.

Back at the theater, Julian showed me the workshop, a padlocked shed behind the theater with a bench and a decent set of tools. He handed me a rough sketch of the set he wanted made from plywood. I needed to shape it and join it so it could be assembled. Some of the others would paint it when I was finished.

"It's for the trial of the Knave of Hearts," he explained. "This will be the jury box and the queen's throne."

"Maybe I can be the Knave of Hearts," I said.

"Lars is our knave for now. Maybe for you, a knight. Just now, you're our carpenter. Get to work!" he passed me a fat joint and left me alone, which was more than fine with me.

As I measured the wood and cut it, I fought with the urge to walk away from Julian and his craziness. I'd never heard of Charles Manson then. I didn't even know the word *cult,* but I knew Julian had some kind of hold over the troupe that was spooky. The other kids obeyed his every word. But why not? Julian had endless supplies of good dope. He treated the girls well, and every guy had a girl, sometimes two of them, whenever he wanted one. If Uncle Sam had offered as good a deal, I would never have left the Army.

I figured I'd stay with Julian a little longer. I wouldn't let his horseshit drive me away.

I could leave whenever I wanted to.

* * *

I worked 'til past midday, then knocked off to look for the others and found the theater empty. I was starving. Julian hadn't given me the key to the shop's padlock and I hated to leave it open, but I figured it would be okay if I grabbed a quick bite at Red's. The worried look in the waitress' eyes had nagged me all morning, so I closed the door tightly and made my way to the diner.

Velma came straight to me. She was pretty and maybe not as old as I had first thought, like the lines around her eyes and mouth came more from smiling than from age. She smiled now as she took my burger order, but I saw the same concern in her eyes. When she brought the food back, I took the plunge.

"Something on your mind?" I asked pleasantly.

She looked around the sparsely occupied room, gave a nod to the other waitress and plopped down on the stool beside mine.

"None of my business," she said, "but I'm kinda surprised you've taken up with Julian and his bunch. You don't seem like an actor or a dancer."

"I'm the... a carpenter," I said. "I took that job."

"I figured, but his last carpenter was an actor too, and a singer. He sang really pretty."

I saw she was holding back, so I asked, "What happened to him?"

"He's... You might've seen him. He's still around. The local cops don't have much use for panhandlers, but I guess he doesn't really ask people for money and they haven't gotten sick enough of him to run him off. I think they feel sorry for him."

I knew she was talking about the gray-faced bum I had seen a couple of times since I hit town.

"What happened to him?"

"Can't say for sure. One day he seemed fine, then I didn't see him with the others for a few days, then next time I did, he was like he is now." She smiled when she looked away. "He had a really nice singing voice."

An overdose of something, I thought, but I just nodded. I'd done enough dex to know what being strung out felt like and, of course, I had read all the stories about LSD and what it could do to your head. One pill makes you smaller, another makes you crazy. "Do you know his name?"

"Bill maybe, but Julian always called him Brilly. You seem like a nice guy. I'd hate to see you get in trouble with..." She didn't finish the sentence, but I understood well enough.

"I'll be careful, Velma," I told her, smiled as reassuringly as I could, and she patted my hand and went back to waiting on tourists. When she brought my burger, it was world-class, though I hardly tasted it. I left her a dollar tip and gave her a wink and a smile as I headed back to finish my work.

As soon as I closed the Fantasia door behind me, I relit the joint Julian had left me, wondering if the troupe had returned. Listening as I passed through the theater, I heard nothing besides creaks and stage ghosts. The pot turned my legs a little rubbery, but I knew I'd be fine once I got to work.

Where were the others? On the beach, I guessed, with a little pang of lonely anger. Was this Julian's way of making me take a part in the play? Or maybe he really needed the sets done that day so they could be painted before the weekend. I didn't have more than another two hours' work and I was already planning the cuts and joints as I walked out of the theater toward the work shed, opened the door and stepped into darkness.

Someone kicked the door out of my hand, slamming it. Combat instincts came back in a stoned rush as I swung into the absolute black and missed.

"Don't," a voice hissed, rasping and desperate, but not threatening. "I just want to talk."

I reached for the light switch, but the voice repeated, "Don't."

I smelled him then, over the cut-wood tang and the stale dope smoke. He stank like cat pee and rotten fruit.

"Brilly?" I guessed.

He grew very still and, as my eyes adjusted to the darkness, I saw his shape and knew I'd guessed right.

"Not Brilly," he corrected me. "Brillig. 'Twas brillig, and the slithy toves...'"

I waited for him to start making sense. I remembered the knife rack, and my hand found the handle of a big carving knife. The hair at the base of my neck stood up and I sensed the imminence of blood.

Brillig sang, his voice just as nice as Velma had described it, "He took his vorpal sword in hand: long time the manxome foe he sought—" Then he watched me in the near darkness. "You don't know the song." He sounded disappointed. "But you will, one way or another. Julian will *show* you."

"Not me, man. There's nothing Julian can show me."

"I thought so too." Brillig giggled. "And here I am."

"He didn't make you a bum. You did that to yourself."

He made a grunting, growling sound. "Now I can't be too near people," he said when he found his voice. "You don't know what it's like, but you will. One way or another." To punctuate his words, he opened the shed door, startling me with how close he had crept in utter silence. I gripped the knife, more than ready to use it.

I let him go, leaving a rank wake behind him as he shuffled across the courtyard and into the alley. Just as he reached the shadows, he looked back over his shoulder, and called out, "'Beware the Jabberwock, my son.'"

In the sudden afternoon light, I saw his face gone almost to bones, skin stretched and pitted, his eyes dancing mad foxfire when they caught the sun. He smiled, and I must have hallucinated, because it seemed like he had double rows of teeth.

* * *

I finished the sets in an anxious blaze, focusing my tensions into the saw and the drill. I worked warily, facing the open door of the shed, but Brillig didn't return. When I finished, barely an hour later, I closed up the shed and locked it. I figured if Julian didn't have the key, he could break the fucking door down.

Just to be on the safe side, I took the carving

knife with me, wrapped its blade with cloth and stuck it in my pocket. I'd get a clasp knife soon, or maybe a gun, and if that fucker Brillig came near me again, I'd be ready. The theater still echoed emptily, so I headed down the boardwalk, rigid with nerves. Julian's pot had done nothing to calm me. I vibrated with paranoid intensity, trying not to look at the tourists as I passed them, afraid of what I would see in their eyes, or what they might see in mine.

When I got to the end of the boardwalk, I remembered what Velma had told me that first morning, that a bunch of the local kids lived at an old hotel, the Marlin, on East 38. I started the Galaxy and sprayed sandy gravel as I hit the blacktop, weaving eastward among the Winnebagos and Airstreams. Past the town limits, I saw the Marlin on the right side of the highway, behind a broken neon sign with a tailless, smiling fish, and an asphalt parking lot full of sorry cars and Julian's rabbit-branded bus. Behind the motel, a line of low, grass-spotted dunes marked the edge of the beach.

When I had climbed out of the Galaxy, I saw, beyond the parking lot, a line of weathered, coral-pink cottages and, beyond them, a swimming pool shining under a couple of sunburned palms. Laughter and music swelled from the cottages, and hippies cavorted in primeval abandon all around the pool, tribal dancing to amped whoops of electronic noise, feedback from a tormented Gibson. I followed the siren's call and saw Julian's troupe at the center of the orgy, a dance of naked frenzy.

It was more than just Julian and the Fantasia

players. There must have been twenty or thirty kids in the dance, most of them bare-assed. Sheena spun out of the sweaty storm and caught me in a hard hug, rubbing her breasts against me, licking my neck. She tore my shirt and bit me just under my nipple; she drew me with her teeth into the dance.

Someone gave me a joint, and the pot bloomed, scattering my fear, rendering it irrelevant. I felt the music throb, my cock hardening as Sheena stroked it through my jeans, her lips red with the trickle of my blood, her tongue teasing my nipple.

We danced, vertical fucking to the crazy noise, and then she pulled me breathless and insane, out of the dance, to Julian.

He handed me a glass of crystalline liquid. "Drink me," he said.

I drained the glass. Sheena's hands worked in my pants now, jacking me. I tried to meet Julian's gaze, but he smiled and looked away. The dance had disintegrated into knots of people sprawled around the pool in inventive patterns of mutual orgasm.

Sheena's hands insisted, and all my anger and tension melted under her touch, the extremity of sensation burning new fire as she pulled me down to the ground, stripped away my jeans and took my cock in her hands. I had never been so hard.

She sat on me sure and fast, impaling herself and riding wild, until she came with a scream of pure abandon. I stayed hard, the world beginning to shimmer, my breath bright light, the space above me arced, the sky a ceiling and Julian's face looking down, beatific, his cock hanging over me, until Sheena leaned out to take him between her lips. She ground down on me, gripped with the wet heat of her cunt, pulled me up into her, until she came in shattering colors, Julian's spunk on her chin, then all of us together, in the moment, the golden glow of perfect orgasm.

Wonderland.

My anxiety uncoiled slowly, like a snake in winter, and Julian must have felt it because he kissed Sheena and told her to leave. I sat up, aware of how close I was to him. He was heavy, but the weight of his naked body appeared solid, not flabby. His cock must have been eight inches long, even spent. I reached for my pants, stood up and slipped them on, carefully checking to be sure I still had the knife.

My heartbeat shook my ribs, and the sky turned entirely to shades of gold and brown. What had he given me? LSD? Something stronger?

Julian put his pants on too and ordered quietly, "Come." My feet moved like he was pulling their strings, like I was nothing more than a tripping marionette. I followed him away from the moans and the cries of the kids, all of them fucking and high.

We walked past the cabins, afternoon sun turning everything to crystals, the weedy grass on the dunes twitching and pulsing with the rhythm of wind and my own blood. As we cleared the last of the buildings, I saw Lorina—Julian's Alice—waiting for us, wearing a short, white skirt and a bikini top to match. Her eyes were black saucers, and her smile was sweet and open.

Julian kissed her cheek and said, "Come and walk with us." He gave me her right hand to hold, and then he took her left and led us both into the dunes, toward the laughing splendor of the sea.

"This has been a good day," he told me. "We rehearsed the play for the brothers and sisters who live here, and now they see with new eyes that Wonderland is all around us if we want it, that the hang-ups and hassles of the world don't matter unless you let them."

"You got them high," I said. "That's all."

Julian laughed, his bare belly shaking with amusement. "Oh what will it take to convince you?" he said, as much to the wind as to me.

The three of us walked barefoot through the sand, up the sloping, warm dune to its crest, then down toward the beach. A nearly flat surf sparkled in breaker lines, foaming on the shore, washing soapy white, then gone again.

"Paradise is ours for the taking, Tom." He embraced me, his bare, sturdy flesh against mine, still holding Lorina's hand. She broke the grip and put her arms around both of us. I saw the moon like a faded ghost on the horizon, a pale, hopeless sphere. Lorina smelled like honey and roses, and my cock grew hard when she laid her hands on my shoulders and back. Julian turned me toward her, and I drowned in the dazzling gold of her hair, in the depthless pits of her eyes.

Alice kissed me, and her lips were life itself, the promise of the world that I had earned by my survival, as precious and arousing as any kiss I ever tasted, her tongue tasting me and pushing deeper, inviting a duel. I crushed her to me. She felt as ethereal as a woman in a dream, a specter of infinite desire.

I loved her more than any woman I had ever loved, and I wanted her with my soul.

She drew me down, Julian helping me because the sand beneath my feet felt treacherous as slippery glass. Together they removed my pants, and Lorina lifted her skirt to show me a tangle of golden hair and the glistening cleft of her cunt. I moved over her, intending to fuck her, but Julian put his hands on my shoulders and pushed me down.

"With your mouth," Alice said, and she widened her legs so I saw her pussy lips and the wetness between them.

I had never gone down on a girl before that night. She smelled sweet, a little like vanilla, as I touched my nose to the ash-pale curls above her pussy. The afternoon light glowed golden around us, and I pressed my lips against her cleft, then the tip of my tongue tentatively at first, until I tasted her. Sweet as honeysuckle, slippery. I pushed deeper, opening her, my tongue finding complexities, folds of flesh, an evasive knot I knew was called a clitoris.

Her scent and slick heat amazed me. I had a lysergic vision of the first ocean pouring out of the cunt of a mother goddess, and I drank it from Alice, even as Julian reached under me and took hold of my cock.

I'd never been touched by a guy before, but it seemed right and natural. I hadn't known I could be so erect without my cock splitting its skin. Julian handled me with rough expertise, jacking my shaft and lifting my arousal to new heights. Alice—Lorina—moaned, and I echoed her when Julian's thumb brushed my asshole.

Lorina was the lush land below the earth and Julian the sky god manifest in the wizard, the mathematician, his lust measured and ruler-exact, his touch upon materiality hot and irresistible.

Lorina began to cry out as my tongue and lips attacked her clit mercilessly. The rhythm was mine now, the same as the sea, the wind, the pulse in the sand, reverberations all the way to the heart of the world. Something cool and gooey creamed my rectum, then the thick head of Julian's cock penetrated me, the sky god claiming the red horizon. Of course he knew the rhythm, and he fucked me, sliding in and out of my ass in glorious, pulsing strokes as he worked my cock with his hand. Alice came, her legs wrapping my head, her hands tangled in my hair as my senses burned between gifts and giving.

She moved against me until she lost the breath to scream, and, beyond her, I saw the sea turn to fire, felt the gush of my own orgasm over Julian's relentless hand and felt him claim me, wet and hot, as he came.

We collapsed and shifted, then lay in the sand together, Lorina between us. My mind whirled and spread upon the dusk, but there was no shame, no regret, only wonder.

"Remember what I have showed you," Julian whispered against my ear. "We are gods, all of us. We can be whatever we allow ourselves to be. Now, there is an important question I must ask you. Consider your answer carefully."

I waited, watching the ocean whitecaps trace sunset fire.

Julian began to giggle. He seemed to suppress the

laughter at first, then gave way to it, merry and open. Lorina laughed too, until I couldn't help myself and laughed with them.

We laughed until the sea stopped burning.

Then he found his voice and asked, still breathless, "So, Carpenter, how did you like the oyster?"

* * *

Thing about acid is, sometimes you can't sleep for hours. After we left the beach, I wandered away by myself. The cascade of color and sensation faded into gray and pearl. I embraced the encounter and accepted. I believed Julian and I thought I understood the lesson of his wonderland. So simple and so hard.

Julian had shown me true freedom.

I found a mat in one of the old motel rooms and stretched, watching the shadows crawl in pastel patterns until flickering darkness claimed the ceiling and then my eyes. I slept deep and without dreaming.

On Saturday, I watched the matinee premier of *Alice, Baby!* from backstage, numb and placid with hashish. I had not seen the costumes before, had not seen the troupe in its glory, razor-sharp in the delivery of their lines, each dance step perfect and professional. Every worn seat held a tourist; pudgy parents and wide-eyed kids. Sheena told me the evening crowd would be hippies, teenagers and younger couples, and there would be joints passed down the rows. When I wasn't mesmerized by the vibrant motion on stage, I watched the faces of the audience, frowns on some of them, but most as entranced as I felt, caught in the glamour of Julian's vision.

Alice danced better than anyone else, animated and innocent. I remembered how she'd tasted and how she'd screamed. I couldn't wait to be with her again.

Near the end of the performance, two of the Waling cops, a big one and a little one, came into the theater and stood at the back.

"Stuff and nonsense," Alice said on the stage. "The idea of having the sentence first."

"Hold your tongue," cried the Queen.

"I won't!"

"Off with her head!"

The two cops looked at each other.

"Who cares for you?" Alice shouted. "You're nothing but a pack of cards."

The dancers whirled in a hallucinogenic rainbow, catching Alice and the Queen up in their frenzy, spinning them, then all collapsing in a heap as the liquid, psychedelic lights dimmed to blackness absolute; even the exit signs extinguished for a moment.

Alice's voice, Lorina's voice, amplified and muted into an enormous whisper that settled on the hall like a veil. "Oh! I've had such a curious dream!"

Then the lights came back up, and the tourists clapped and whistled before they shuffled to their feet and out into the afternoon sun, but the cops stayed until the audience had gone. As they came toward the stage, I looked around and realized everyone else had split too.

"What's your name?" the big cop asked.

"Tom Rimer."

He had a few more questions, and I answered them honestly.

"Soldier boy, eh?" the little one asked. He was older, and I wasn't surprised when he said, "My boy's over there. Don't suppose you knew him, Danny Breshca? He's an MP."

"No, sir," I told him. "I was mostly in the boonies."

After that, both officers treated me with polite respect. I wondered if Julian had left me to talk to them because he knew they would.

"You know a guy named Bill O'Daniel?"

I started to say no.

"They call him Brilly."

"Yeah," I said. "I've met him. Why?"

"He's wanted for almost killing a woman this morning. Velma, waitress at Red's next door."

"Damn." My chest constricted. "Is she okay?"

"She will be. She's at the hospital up in Ludville. Lost a lot of blood. Looks like the guy tried to take her head off, but she fought him and some fishermen came along. She was lucky."

"He cut her?" My pot-bemused glow had blossomed into an adrenalin rush.

"No, Tom. He used his teeth."

* * *

When the cops went away, I looked for Julian, but he'd left the theater. Most of the troupe avoided me, like the aura of cop heat had rubbed off on me. I told Sheena what the officers had said, and she shivered and hugged me.

I understood that all of them were afraid, but whether of Brilly or Julian, I couldn't say.

The evening performance played to a half-empty house, and we all knew why. The whole town buzzed with evil rumor. Two fishermen had vanished from a secluded cove; a little girl had been attacked.

Already the boardwalk seemed deserted.

After the late show closed, we sat in the big room behind the stage, drinking warm wine. No one passed a pipe or joint because we all knew the cops were watching, probably sniffing at the doors eager to make a bust.

Julian sprawled on one of the mattresses. "It's all right," he said. "Maybe we'll move along and come back next summer. We'll give it a few more weeks."

I spoke as calmly as I could. "What did you do to him, Julian?"

The room tensed. Sheena caught my arm with sharp nails.

But Julian answered, calm and thoughtful, "Hmm? To Brillig? We did nothing to him. He is what he wants to be. Jabberwocks are the price of Wonderland, you see?"

As usual, Julian's words made no sense.

"What are you going to do about him?" I asked.

"Me?" Julian asked. I heard chuckles and suppressed giggles. He reached down, under the mattress and drew out a knife, the carving knife from the shed. My knife. He handed it to me, and I accepted it from him. He hugged me, and I felt a sweetly painful ache when we kissed. "There's your Vorpal blade," he said. "Now go kill the Jabberwock."

The hilt felt good in my hand. I thought about Velma, how frightened she must have been. I saw myself stalking Brillig in the darkness, almost smelled his stink there in the room with us. I stood up slowly, more aware than anyone else of just how closely their Jabberwock lurked.

I held the blade and studied my reflection in its steel. The Army gave me a gun and orders to kill. My family and town constructed conventional walls to cage me. Julian gave me choice.

I tossed the blade lightly so its point stuck in the old wooden floor between me and Julian. I loved Julian with all my soul and I would thank him every day of my life for what he had shown me.

But I was a free man and I wouldn't kill for him.

"Not me," I told him. "I've done that. You kill your own goddamn Jabberwock."

Then I walked out of the Theatre de Fantasia and I tried with all my soul never to look back.

* * *

Of course, it wasn't that easy.

They never caught Brillig, but I had to go back to Waling three times to answer questions. The second time, well into October, the Theatre de Fantasia stood empty, its marquee blank. Officer Breshca told me the bus had rolled out a week earlier, the troupe headed for Mexico. I thought a long time about following them, but I went home instead.

A year later, I was living in New Orleans and a package came in the mail. Even before I had peeled the wrapping away, I recognized the contents. My knife. The Vorpal blade, and a note. *"You may need this yet. Love, Julian."*

I owe Julian a debt I can never repay. He freed me, and for almost forty years, I've lived just like he showed me. I've loved men and women and embraced colorful ecstasy and bright hope. I cherish the wonderland that is this world. He opened my mind, and I live every day free in my heart and my soul.

I saw Julian all through the eighties, late at night, on high-numbered cable channels, selling his vision for a penny less than twenty bucks. Brightstar Ministries. Now he's on the Internet. Thousands of people follow him.

Sometimes I think about going to him, telling him how much he did for me, offering to give him my freedom like a sacrifice, but then I remember I am free.

And I keep my Vorpal blade sharp and near.

Contributors

Holly Abair writes just about anything that jumps into her head, from romance to nonfiction and everywhere along the road. She lives in the middle of the woods somewhere in Massachusetts. When Holly is not at the computer playing with her imaginary friends, she can usually be found sketching, dancing, doing glasswork or in an overstuffed armchair with a good book and a cup of tea.

J. Blackmore is a quiet, cat-loving editor living in the wilds of Canada. No, really. She is the editor of many anthologies of erotica riffing on English literature and themes including *Sense and Sensuality* (Jane Austen), *Elementary Erotica* (Sherlock Holmes), *The Circlet Treasury of Erotic Steampunk*, and many more. Her next project is an anthology of Jules Verne-themed erotica.

Angela Caperton is the author of *Man's World*, an erotic novel of manners and space travel. Her eclectic erotica spans many genres, including romance, horror, fantasy and what she calls contemporary-with-a-twist. Look for her stories published with Cleis, Circlet Press, Drollerie

Press, eXtasy Books, and in the indie magazine *Out of the Gutter*. Visit Angela at http://blog.angelacaperton.com.

Morwenna Drake was born in Cornwall but has since migrated north to Yorkshire. She lives in a very ordinary house, nothing like the castles and mansions which dominate her imagination. When not writing or daydreaming, she enjoys creative crafts such as sewing or cookery, and playing the piano. She memorized the poetry of Carroll as a child and to this day can still recite "Jabberwocky" without hesitation (although no one ever asks her to).

ADR Forte is the author of the erotic short story collection *Touch of Steel*. Her erotic stories appear in numerous anthologies including *Like an Animal* and *Like a Queen*. Her tales of erotic fantasy can be found in collections from Cleis Press and Circlet Press. http://www.adrforte.com.

Much to his embarrassment, **Bernie Mojzes** has outlived Lord Byron, Percy Shelley, Janice Joplin and the Red Baron, without even once having been shot down over Morlancourt Ridge. Having failed to achieve a glorious martyrdom, he has instead turned his hand to the penning of paltry prose (a rather wretched example of which you currently hold in your hands), in the pathetic hope that he shall here find the notoriety that has thus far proven elusive. Should Pity, or perhaps a Perverse Curiosity move you to seek him out, he can be found at http://www.kappamaki.com.

Verity Penvenen was born in Sunderland but now lives in splendid isolation on the Northumbrian coast. Apart from a few sheep and chickens, her main companion is her black cat, Moth. She enjoys painting in both oils and acrylics and is sometimes a life-model, which allows her to sit quietly and think up plot and character ideas. She loves Lewis Carroll and has a whole bookshelf devoted to every copy of Alice she can find.

Alex Picchetti knows that a good superhero must always be wary of villains and so cannot reveal her day job. She lives near Toronto with her three spoiled cats.

Theresa Sand has a weakness for good books, museums and Andes chocolate mints. You can read more about her misadventures on her blog theresasand.wordpress.com.

Gary Westfahl is the author, editor or coeditor of 24 books about science fiction and fantasy, including the Hugo Award-nominated *Science Fiction Quotations* (2005) and *The Greenwood Encyclopedia of Science Fiction and Fantasy* (2005), as well as hundreds of articles, book and film reviews and reference book entries. However, his wife and family are always urging him to write fiction in order to earn more money.

If You Liked This Title, You Might Also Like:

The Circlet Treasury of Erotic Steampunk
Edited by J. Blackmore & Cecilia Tan

*The Circlet Treasury of Lesbian Erotic Science
Fiction and Fantasy*
Edited By Cecilia Tan

*The Siren and the Sword:
Book One of the Magic University Series*
By Cecilia Tan

*The Tower and the Tears:
Book Two of the Magic University Series*
By Cecilia Tan

*The Incubus and the Angel:
Book Three of the Magic University Series*
By Cecilia Tan

Spellbinding: Tales from Magic University
Edited by Cecilia Tan

*The Poet and The Prophecy
Book Four of the Magic University Series*
By Cecilia Tan